D1232629

Hard Candy

Amanda Young

HARD CANDY

Acknowledgements

This book is dedicated to all the readers who requested the Candy series in print. You guys rock!

Contents

Man Candy

Chapter One

The sun shone brightly, not a single cloud daring to mar the baby-blue perfection of the sky. Not quite eight a.m., it was already close to eighty degrees. A perfect Monday morning for Aaron Samuels's daily walk to work. Living less than a mile from both his job and college, he'd never seen the point of buying a car. With his meager salary as an administrative assistant at Remora's Construction, he could scarcely afford the upkeep and insurance anyway.

Under his breath, he whistled a song, some little ditty about love and loss he'd heard on the radio before leaving home. His sneakers made good time over the cracked sidewalk, drawing him closer to his place of employment.

On his way in, he passed by a Starbucks and was tempted to buy himself a cappuccino or one of those frothy drinks everyone on TV always raved about. A quick tally in his head of the amount of money he had left for the month, and he changed his mind. He could wait for a plain old regular cup of coffee once he got into the office. That wouldn't cost him anything, and it was just as good. No sense in spending money when he didn't have to.

He smiled good morning at a middle-aged woman in cutoffs and T-shirt who speed-walked passed him, a tiny Chihuahua on a leash in front of her. With a glance both ways, he jogged across the road and picked up his pace.

Not usually a morning person, today he was happy and chipper as could be. Things were beginning to look up for him. In the past month, he'd aced his final exams and graduated in the top ten percent of his class with a degree in horticulture. On the recommendation of his counselor, he'd dared to reach for the stars and had applied for management positions at several companies and nurseries. He was surprised to hear back from Lowe's within two weeks. He'd made it through the grueling interview—something he'd never been good at—and landed a job as floor manager over the garden department.

Aaron approached the squat brick building that housed the Remora's Construction office and entered through the dingy glass door. He made a mental note to grab some glass cleaner to take care of the smudges. Cleaning wasn't in his job description, but appearances could make all the difference in how a business was perceived. He didn't mind going above the call of duty for his boss. Logan Remora was a great man to work for, had been exceedingly kind to Aaron over the four years he'd worked as Logan's assistant, and Aaron didn't mind doing a little extra now and then, if it helped make things run more smoothly for the man. It was the least he could do, especially now that he would be putting in his notice.

A disconcerting ball of sadness formed in the pit of his gut at the thought of moving on and leaving his current position. He'd grown comfortable at Remora's Construction and didn't look forward to starting over elsewhere, though he had to admit that he was excited about the raise he would garner. The increased salary would be more than appreciated by someone who lived off of Ramen Noodles and Pop-Tarts a lot of the time.

2

What he didn't look forward to was leaving his boss short-handed at the end of the week. He would've liked to have given more notice, but the new job required he begin next Monday, and he wasn't about to start out a new position on the wrong foot by trying to wheedle for more time. He just hoped he didn't put Mr. Remora in a bind.

Aaron stopped midway down the short hall between two identical doors, one with blue, curlicue lettering spelling out Interior Design by Jake, the other with straight black script declaring Remora's Construction.

Twisting to his right, he unlocked the door leading into Remora's Construction and stepped inside, locking it back up behind him for the time being. Mr. Remora's twin brother, Jake, owned the interior design company. While the brothers ended up working together on several projects a year, they both seemed to prefer to keep their businesses separate. Which didn't make a whole lot of sense to Aaron, considering the overhead and other costs, but as a lowly assistant, he didn't have any right to tell anyone how to run their company. His job was to make coffee and fetch files, not to tell them how to improve their business efficiency. Or, it would be his job for the rest of the week. After that, he was on to bigger and better things.

He dreamed of having his own landscape design business one day. This was why he'd majored in horticulture and minored in business. With his degree, he would be able to handle the design aspects and the office. A bit of a control freak, he didn't like the thought of depending on someone else to do that work for him. Although he probably would have to hire some help, some little flunky not unlike himself, to do all the things he didn't care for, such as answering the phones.

The thought put a smile on his face as he bypassed the drab front room—occupied by his small desk in one corner, and a grouping of four chairs and a table littered with an assortment of old magazines in another—and walked into the tiny kitchenette. There he busied himself with making a fresh pot of coffee, the special dark roast his boss liked best, before returning to his desk and checking to see if there were any messages on the machine.

He scribbled down a couple of messages about scheduling an appointment for estimates on work, and another from Jake, reminding his brother about some after-hours business meeting they had to attend later in the week. He booted up his computer, an old dinosaur of a desktop, so it could warm up while he went out to clean the filthy glass doors. He ran into the bathroom and grabbed a roll of paper towels and a half-full spray-bottle of glass cleaner from beneath the sink before heading out. As he stepped out the door, he once again glanced across the hall at the pretty design on Jake's door. Logan should do something more like that on his entrance, he thought, instead of sticking with plain black lettering. Jake's was so much more appealing.

Aaron shook his head, shaggy auburn hair falling over onto his forehead, and misted the glass with cleaner. He tore off a fistful of towels and wiped down the glass, using long, smooth strokes to keep it from streaking.

Sometimes it was really hard to remember that Logan and Jake were related, much less identical twins. Each man was attractive, with thick dark hair, eyes so deep brown they bordered on black, and a naturally tan complexion that hinted at their Mediterranean heritage, but those basic features were where the things they had in common ended. Everything else about them was polar opposite. Jake was friendly and artistic, always very proper about things, and supposedly as gay as the day was long, though Aaron had never seem him with either sex outside of business. Logan was the embodiment of exactly what someone would expect a general contractor to be: rough around the edges, a bit uncouth at times, but an overall nice guy. He even married his high school sweetheart right after graduation and was still married to her.

Which made the way Aaron felt about Logan all the more inappropriate and uncomfortable. It was true that people had no control over who they fell in love with, because he'd been in love with his boss for the last four years. No matter how many dates he'd gone on, or how many men he'd let fuck him

4

into oblivion, the hopeless yearning he felt for a man he could never have would not go away.

Thank God he wouldn't have to worry about having temptation so near after the end of the week. His greatest fear was that Logan would somehow find out his secret and confront him about it. He would shrivel up and die if that happened. It was one thing to be attracted to someone straight, another thing to be attracted to your boss, or even a married man. All those things combined, however, were a nightmare waiting to happen, the equivalent of when he'd had his pants yanked down in front of the entire sixth-grade class by that bully, Mike what's-his-name. That one still haunted his dreams on occasion.

A rough hand slapped down on Aaron's shoulder. He jumped and spun around, dropping the paper towels to the ground, where they unceremoniously unrolled out over the slate-grey linoleum.

"Hey, Aaron, calm down. It's just me. I didn't mean to scare ya."

Aaron tilted his head up and stared into Jake's eyes, a shade lighter than ink, and felt himself relax a tad. The defensive set of his shoulders eased, and he took a relieved breath. "Shit. How many times have I asked you not to sneak up on me?"

Jake laughed, the heavy rumble building up from deep in his broad chest. A chest currently covered in a salmon-colored shirt—silk, if Aaron guessed right—and coupled with a stiffly pressed pair of beige Dockers. Knowing Jake, the shirt was probably from some obscure fashion designer no one had ever heard of. He was like that. Always up on whatever the latest up-and-comer was producing. Not for the first time, Aaron wondered why he couldn't have fallen for Jake. He didn't have a snowball's chance in hell of landing either of them, not a skinny, freckled little nerd like him, but somehow being rejected by Jake seemed like less of a tragedy than the unrequited feelings he harbored for Logan. At least with Jake he could've made a move and been shot down. That was probably half his problem right there—without being able to express his feelings for Logan, they coalesced into a huge, over exaggerated ball inside him and festered there with no way out. He hoped that was the problem, anyway. With time and distance, he was sure the feelings would dissipate. He hated to think otherwise. Endlessly carrying a torch for someone he couldn't be with was too torturous a thought to contemplate.

"Sorry, bud. I called out to you, but you were a million miles away. Must've been thinking about something good, too, because I know washing the windows isn't that damn interesting."

Aaron rolled his eyes. "Oh, it is. I have a secret fetish for windows. Like to spend my free time jerking off on them. You just caught me cleaning up my mess before the big boss man comes in."

Jake chuckled and slapped him playfully on the shoulder. "You're too much, Aaron. I'm going to miss seeing your cute face around here when you finally land a job with that spiffy new degree of yours."

Aaron felt heat suffuse his face, both at the offhand compliment and the reference to his leaving. With his fair complexion, he imagined his face was the color of beets. Blushing was one of the many downfalls of being a natural redhead. "Yeah, about that, I—"

"About what?" Logan breezed through the entrance door and strolled up to them in his usual uniform of tight, worn denim and a faded company T-shirt stretched across his wide shoulders. His obsidian gaze traveled back and forth between Aaron and Jake. "Don't you have anything better to do with your time than stand around harassing my help, Jake?"

Aaron couldn't help himself. He visually devoured every ridge of muscle in his boss's chest and abdomen, clearly delineated in form-fitting black cotton. The jeans hung precariously low on his narrow hips, as if a stiff wind would blow them down at any second. Aaron would have given his eyeteeth to see that happen just once.

Logan cleared his throat, and Aaron realized he'd been caught staring, which, in turn, made his face flame even hotter. He sputtered, "Uh, what were you saying, Mr. Remora?"

"I asked if Jake was bothering you."

"Uh, no. We were just talking."

Logan's gaze seemed to soften. "Good. How about some coffee, Aaron? And how many times do I have to remind you to call me Logan? You'd think you would be comfortable enough to call me by name by now. You've been under me forever."

Don't I wish? The only time I've ever been under you is in my fantasies, and I call out your name plenty in those. Aaron felt his face heat up at his wayward thoughts.

Jake smirked. "Told ya, I wasn't bothering the kid. I was just telling him that we're going to miss him when he leaves."

"Leaves?" Logan turned those perceptive eyes toward Aaron. "Have you found another position already?"

Shit. This was so not the way he wanted to give his notice. He'd imagined a whole little speech where he told Logan how much he'd enjoyed working for him and about a hundred other things that completely flew out of his brain while he had two identical sets of eyes curiously staring at him and waiting for an answer. He felt like he was under a microscope. Naked, under a microscope, and falling short of expectation.

Aaron resisted the urge to squirm. "I, um, was just about to tell Jake here that I accepted a position with Lowe's."

"That's fuckin' great, man. I bet you're thrilled." Jake clapped him on the back again. A little harder this time, almost too forcefully, because he listed to the side a bit, his shoulder brushing over Logan's arm. Little tingles crawled down his arm and made his fingers itch to reach out and squeeze the corded muscular forearm within his reach. God, he was pitiful. He really needed to get a life.

He glanced up at Logan, curious about how he'd taken the news, and found an odd expression on his face. Logan caught his gaze and nodded. "That's great. Congratulations. When are you supposed to start?"

"Uh, well, about that..." His gaze shot down, and he pretended to pluck lint off his polo shirt. He tried to pick and choose his words, but nothing came to him. Better to spit it all out and get it over with. "You see, they want me to start right away, so I'll only be able to finish out this week. Friday will be my last day. I'm sorry."

Aaron glanced back up. Logan was studying his face like there was something hanging out of his nose. His hand rose to make sure there wasn't. Logan nodded. "Sure, no problem. I'm sure I can get a temp agency to send someone out."

"Thanks, Mr., err, Logan. If you'd like, I could call for you and see if they'd be able to send someone out early, so I can walk them through how you like things."

"Yeah, that'd be good, Aaron. Thank you. About that coffee?"

Aaron knew a dismissal when he heard one. "Coming right up." He turned and ducked into the office. Before the door closed behind him, he could have sworn he heard Logan telling Jake to stay away from his assistant.

Weird.

He'd have to remember to assure Logan that Jake wasn't bothering him. He liked talking to Jake. The man had a zany sense of humor. As he poured coffee into Logan's favorite Virginia Tech mug, he decided just to pretend he hadn't heard anything. With him leaving at the end of the week, it was a moot point anyway.

Chapter Two

Tuesday turned out to be a nasty, dreary day. Angry clouds obscured the sky and threatened rain for the better part of the morning. As promised on Monday evening, the temp agency sent someone around noon. Unfortunately, the woman—and he used that term lightly because she couldn't have been a day over eighteen—they sent must have thought she was on some blind date reality show. She spent what little time she was there ignoring Aaron's attempts to teach her anything about the position, choosing instead to bat her eyelashes at Logan every chance she got.

Thankfully—because her feeble attempts to get Logan's attention grated on his nerves—his boss was out of the office for the majority of the day, on one call or another, doing estimates for potential clients. At five on the dot, Aaron happily sent Bimbo Barbie home and placed a call to the agency, informing them that her services were no longer needed. Since he didn't want to get her in trouble with her employer, he made up a lame excuse about her not being qualified for the position instead of telling them that she was completely incompetent. They offered to re-screen their potential candidates and send someone else.

He hoped whomever they sent would work out, because he was running out of time. His job wasn't hard, but there were a lot of little details he wanted to pass along. All the odds and ends that made the business and Logan's schedule run smoother. Simple things, like how Logan took his coffee, or the best way to take messages so Logan would better understand what was expected of him when he returned calls.

Aaron had run things from behind the scenes for so long, he wanted to make sure all his hard work didn't fall apart without him. It had absolutely nothing to do with wanting to make sure Logan was taken care of. It didn't. Logan had a wife to see to his needs. He didn't need Aaron, his dorky little twink of an assistant, to worry about him.

As if his dismal thoughts caused it, a clap of thunder ripped through the quiet. He turned to the double-paned window bedside his desk in time to see a torrent of rain fall from the sky. Sheets of it splashed against the windowsill and blanketed the landscape outside.

"Great," Aaron mumbled to himself. Call a taxi, which he couldn't really afford, or walk home in the rain. The bus wasn't an option, because the closest stop was over halfway to his apartment. By the time he got there, he would already be soaked.

"What's great?"

Aaron gaze shot to the doorway, where his boss stood just over the threshold. He'd been so lost in thought, staring out the window, that he hadn't heard Logan come in. "Nothing. Just wishing the rain would've waited until after I got home."

Logan closed the door behind him and locked it. Before stepping any further into the room, he glanced around. "Is she gone yet?"

Aaron grinned. Thank God Logan hadn't liked her either. He would've felt bad for canning her. "Long gone. I sent her packing at five."

"I hope you called the agency and told them to send someone else."

"Right before you got here."

"Good. I don't want some woman in here making goo-goo eyes at me all day. It's unnerving." With that, he unbuckled the work belt around his waist and dropped it to the floor. The heavy tools clanked when they hit the beige tile next to Aaron's desk. "Oh, that's better." Logan stretched, pushing his shoulders back. "I swear that damn thing gets heavier every day. Sucks getting old."

Aaron's gaze devoured Logan's beautiful muscular frame. For some reason, all those lean, corded muscles reminded him of a jungle cat preparing to pounce on his prey. And damn if that didn't make him want to drop out of his chair, roll to his back, and expose his belly for sacrifice. Instead, he snorted. "Yep. Thirty-five is decrepit. Next thing you know, you'll need a cane just to hobble in and out of the office."

Logan rolled his eyes, but smiled, little crinkles popping up in the tanned skin around his eyes and mouth. "Smartass." He bypassed Aaron on the way back to his private office. Over his shoulder, he said, "If you want to wait around for a bit, I'll give you a lift home. Can't have you out walking around in the rain and getting sick on me, now can I?"

It was a nice offer. Being in such close quarters with the object of his affection made Aaron spring wood just thinking about it. Accepting wasn't a good idea. His luck, the man would inadvertently rub his thigh while shifting gears and make him go off like a schoolboy. And how mortifying would that be? Better to call a cab and waste a little money. With so little time left, he'd hate to end his current job on a sour note. Coming all over himself more than qualified.

"Thanks anyway," he called after Logan, "but I'm just going to call a cab."

"All right, if you're sure. It's no trouble."

"Don't worry about it," Aaron hollered back. He recognized a trace of stubbornness in his boss's voice, the ability to easily read the man one of the perks that came from having worked together so long.

He picked up the handset and called for a cab before he could be talked out of it.

"My cab's on its way. I'm just going to go out and wait for it in the vestibule." Aaron didn't wait for an answer before heading for the door.

Logan's gravelly voice startled him—so close, when Aaron had believed he was on his way down the hall toward his office. "Aaron. Why don't you stick around for a minute? I'd like to talk to you about something."

Aaron swung back around. His heart skipped a beat at his boss's ominous words. "Um, okay." *Shit.* He moseyed over to his desk, faking a calm he didn't feel, and propped his hip against the corner. "What do you, um, want to talk about?"

Facing him, Logan leaned back against the wall and crossed his thick forearms over his chest. "I couldn't help but notice that there's been a lot of staring and what almost seems like flirting going on lately." He paused and studied Aaron's face.

Flames shot up Aaron's neck and engulfed his cheeks. He dropped his eyes, too ashamed of his behavior to look Logan in the face. What he really wanted to do was crawl under his desk and hide. Logan knew.

"I guess what I'm trying to say is, if the reason you're leaving is because of Jake's teasing you, I've put a stop to it. I had a talk with Jake, and he gave me his word he wouldn't do it anymore."

Aaron jerked his head up and met his boss's eyes. He exhaled. Logan didn't know. *Oh, thank you, God.* Now he didn't have to die of humiliation. "I appreciate that, but Jake doesn't have anything to do with my leaving. I like Jake fine. It's just a better job offer. That's all."

Logan's intense gaze raked over Aaron's face as if he was trying to judge his sincerity. Finally, appearing satisfied with what he saw, Logan smiled. "Okay. I'm glad we cleared the air about that. It was bothering me. Now that we've got that unpleasantness out of the way, I was wondering if there was any way I could change your mind about staying on here. I shouldn't have to tell you that you're going to be missed."

Logan's statement had a more powerful effect on Aaron than Jake's comment yesterday about him being cute. His body skipped the blush and went straight into horny hyperdrive, the tender skin of his balls wrinkling up tight to his groin to make room for his dick to grow. Aaron swallowed a whimper, determined to get through the next few minutes without embarrassing himself.

"That's a tempting offer, but unless you could match the salary and benefits I'd be getting with Lowe's, I'm going to have to move on. I don't really want to, but I'm going to have student loans to repay soon, and, well, the extra cash will be nice. Shoot, they even offer stock options. As much as I've always liked Pop-Tarts, I get sick of eating them for every meal."

Logan's dark eyes widened. "Jesus, Aaron, why didn't you tell me things had gotten so tight? I would've figured out a way to give you a better raise or something."

It wasn't Logan's fault Aaron had chosen to move out of his dorm after his roommate had tried to force him into giving him a blowjob. Or that the reasonable rent he'd agreed to pay had mysteriously gone up six months after he'd moved in. Aaron shrugged. "It's no big deal."

"The hell it's not. I could have done something to help you! You should have come to me."

God, he loved this man. There wasn't a single bad bone in his body. Except for maybe his dick, his stupid, straight dick. "You're my boss. I didn't want to bother you with my problems."

12

A sad look on his face, Logan shook his head. "I thought we were friends. Friends help each other."

He wouldn't know. He didn't really have any, except for Ross, who was the king of being oblivious to anything outside of his own self-obsessed little world. "I guess."

Logan pointed toward the window. "Your ride's here."

Aaron turned to look, and sure enough, a yellow cab was pulled up to the curb, waiting on him. "Guess I better get out there."

Disappointment stamped all over his face, Logan muttered, "Yeah," and turned his back on Aaron. He walked into his office without another word.

A sharp pain shot through Aaron's chest as he left the office. It felt suspiciously like someone twisting a knife in his heart.

* * * * *

Aaron spent his evening at home, in his cramped efficiency apartment with only his host of plants for company. One-sided, rambling conversations abounded as he watered his treasures—a plethora of fern species, an English ivy, and his favorite, a flourishing mother-in-laws tongue—and talked to them about things he'd never tell another soul.

At midnight, feeling tired but restless, Aaron finally stripped down and crawled into bed. Lying on his lumpy futon and unable to sleep, he rolled over onto his back, squeezed his eyelids shut, and imagined he wasn't alone. That the man he loved was beside him, holding him close. If he concentrated hard enough, he could almost feel the ghostly touch of Logan's thick forearms wrapped around him, work-roughened hands exploring his chest and tweaking his nipples.

Said nipples peaked, aching to be touched, and Aaron answered their call, pinching each puckered bit of flesh with just enough pressure to add a sharp bite of pain. Some men didn't have sensitive nipples, but Aaron did. He loved to have them played with, sucked on. He licked a finger and twirled it around one small bud, wishing it was Logan's tongue. Imagining how good it would feel if it were.

Fingertips trailed lightly down the midsection of his torso, gooseflesh rising in their wake. They smoothed over the rise and dip of one hipbone, skirted around his cock, and cupped his balls, rolling them in his palm. He added a bit of pressure, squeezing the delicate orbs lightly.

He placed his feet flat against the bed and spread his legs, pushing up. The hand fondling his nipple digressed and followed its counterpoint down his abs to the base of his cock, ringing it loosely. One last rub to his balls and his fingers moved backward, caressing the soft skin behind them, pressing in on the root of his cock, where it could be felt beneath the skin.

Aaron tilted his head back and bit his lip, losing himself in the sensations wracking his body. In his mind, it wasn't his hands working him to completion, but Logan's.

Contrary thoughts flittered through his mind, interrupting his pleasure for a fraction of a second. What would it be like to fuck someone he loved, who loved him in return? Would Logan be a snuggler and hold him close while they made love?

In Aaron's imagination, he did.

Logan's heat would surround him, his larger body enveloping Aaron's slighter form. With Logan's touch would come an innate sense of belonging, of being part of something bigger than himself. For once, it wouldn't be about the mutual race to get off, but about pleasuring his partner and receiving the same in kind.

Oh, how he longed for that experience.

A soft hand pumped his cock. Fingers fisted around the base of his prick and pulled, adding snug friction. Inching upward, they contracted around the swollen flare of his cockhead and squeezed. The tip of a thumbnail pressed down into the tiny, weeping slit, prompting more moisture to flow. Its pad collected the silky tears and rubbed them over his bulbous cap, teasing the hidden nerves to life before pulling the remaining moisture down his shaft, coating his cock in satiny wetness.

Stroke. Tap. Thumb swirl. Over and over.

The fingers pressing into his perineum moved away. He sucked them into his mouth, wetting them with his saliva. They returned, tips grazing over his hole, teasing.

The taut ring of muscle fluttered emptily, aching to be filled. A single digit filled his need, pressing inside to the first knuckle. His hips lifted, seeking more, and a second joined the first, stretching him open, burning as seldom-used muscles parted and allowed them in deeper, all the way to the webbing.

A low moan bubbled up in his chest and escaped his lips, ricocheting loudly in the still bedroom. The desperate sound echoed back to his ears, driving Aaron to move faster, pump his hips forward and back. Reveling in the feel of a tight fist stroking his cock, the pair of fingers twisting inside him, stret-ching his ass.

Logan's image—his dark penetrating gaze, stern pink lips, and stubborn chin—flashed through the forefront of Aaron's mind and made him whimper. A fingertip glanced over his prostate, making his balls contract and release. Orgasm slammed into him, making him tremble, wracking his body with shudders as his creamy essence spilled over his palm and splattered over his rippling abdomen.

With Logan's name on his lips, Aaron came.

As the final tremors subsided, leaving him weak as a kit-ten, an unintelligible emptiness filled him. His nose began to burn, signaling tears that he forced away by sheer will. His fantasy left him feeling drained and lonely, worse than he'd been to start with.

Chapter Three

On Wednesday, Aaron's workday turned out to be infinite-ly better. The temp agency sent a man, somewhere in his early to mid thirties, named Mark Davis. Thankfully, he turned out to be a quick study. By lunchtime, he was single-handedly running the office, with Aaron's supervision.

For once, Aaron ate his peanut butter and jelly sandwich in peace, without being interrupted by a phone call or a visitor every five minutes. It was a nice change of pace. Or it would have been, if an almost palpable sense of longing hadn't clouded his every thought. Masturbating the night before had left him cranky and out of sorts.

That Logan seemed to be avoiding him, as if he knew what Aaron secretly yearned for night after night, didn't help his state of mind. Other than the morning, when Logan had made an appearance to double check his appointment calendar, Aaron hadn't seen him all day. The man hadn't even called in to check his messages, which was highly unlike him.

Aaron tried to convince himself he was being silly, that he was obsessing and allowing his own frustrated desires to muddy his judgment. Nevertheless, when it neared five o'clock and Logan still hadn't made an appearance, a small part of him felt ostracized. The same contrary part of his psyche that insisted his feelings for Logan were more than lust and were, in fact, love. All consuming, never-ending, up-shit-creek-without-a-paddle love. Something no amount of time or distance would solve. If that were the case, he was sunk, because unless his penis fell off—God forbid—and he magically sprouted a vagina—a scarier thought than losing his dick—his feelings were not going to be reciprocated in this lifetime.

Which only served to reinforce the sad state of his life.

It'd been months since his last failed date; maybe it was time to jump back into the singles mélange and find someone to fuck. Getting laid had never worked before, but with no other options, and his wrist only a couple more jerk-off sessions away from developing an advanced case of carpal tunnel, he needed to do something. Maybe this time he would find someone great, someone who set off all the bells and whistles in his head and made him forget Logan Remora existed. Not likely, but stranger things had happened. Maybe he'd get lucky in more ways than one.

The phone rang, startling him out of his thoughts, something that had been happening more and more lately, and he

16

jerked it up off holder. "Remora's Construction. How may I help you?"

"Aaron?"

"Yeah." It was Ross, his fair-weather friend. He put his hand over the receiver and spoke to Mark, their hopeful new temp. "You can take off if you want." He pointed to the clock, which read ten minutes till five. "Doubt we get any more business today anyway."

Mark smiled and nodded, his neat little bifocal glasses wobbling on the bridge of his nose. "Thanks. See you in the morning?" he asked cautiously.

"Yeah. Eight o'clock. Thanks for coming in."

He watched Mark go while Ross rambled nonstop in his ear. "Thank God you're still at work. I was afraid I wouldn't be able to catch you before you went home. You really need to remember to keep your cell phone on, bud."

"Yeah, sorry about that. So, what's up?" Aaron didn't bother to remind his friend that it wasn't a matter of remembering to turn it on; it was a matter of running out of minutes and not being able to afford to go over his limit. A huge wireless bill would be impossible to pay, and he didn't want to ruin his good credit by getting it cut off.

"How would you feel about going out with me tomorrow night? I pulled some strings and managed to get my name on the guest list for the grand reopening for Evocative Arts, the gallery over on Fifth Street, but my date just called and bailed on me. Something about needing to get his sleep for a big job interview Friday morning or something like that, I forget. Anyway, there's this hot young piece of man candy doing his first showing in honor of the reopening, and I really, really want to go. Do you think you'd be interested? I don't want to go by myself; that would look pathetic. And I figured you're not doing anything anyway, so…what do ya say? Will you go?"

An art gallery? That sounded expensive. "I don't know, Ross. It sounds a little fancy, and I probably don't have anything to wear, and…" He really wasn't all that interested in art. At least, not the kind that would probably be on display. While he enjoyed a nice portrait or landscape, he had no interest in

17

anything abstract. He could never figure out what they were and would only end up offending the artist and/or embarrassing himself when he tried to guess.

"Come on, Aaron. It'll be fun, and I'll even take you out to dinner afterwards, my treat, in exchange for your going with me. Please."

Aaron was just about to cave and agree to go when he heard the unmistakable sound of heavy footsteps outside the office door. Logan. Aaron held his breath. The door crept open and Jake entered, whistling. Aaron blew out a disappointed breath.

Ross's nasal voice sounded in his ear. "Well, will you go?"

Aaron held up a finger at Jake, letting him know he would be off the phone in a second. "Yeah, I'll go with you. Pick me up at my apartment beforehand, okay? Now, I really have to go, Ross. Business calls. See you tomorrow evening."

He disconnected the call and looked toward Jake, who'd pulled over one of the four chairs from across the room and straddled it while Aaron had finished up his call.

Jake grinned. "Hot date tomorrow?"

Aaron rolled his eyes. "No, just a friend in need. He wants me to go to some art show tomorrow. So, what are you doing here? Shouldn't you be off by now?"

"I'm on my way out. Just thought I would drop in and say hi first. And that's too bad about the date, by the way. You should get out more. Socialize."

Aaron barely suppressed his embarrassment over being a social hermit. He didn't feel comfortable at clubs, and there was no way he would be caught dead at any of the private tea rooms or bathhouses he'd heard about. Instead of getting defensive, though, he decided to pick back at Jake. "How do you know I don't? I could have a line of men waiting for me back at my place."

The grin slipped off Jake's face. "I know a couple of men you could have wrapped around your little finger, if you wanted."

"Oh, please. Name them."

"You're looking at one." Jake winked.

Aaron's pulse kicked up a notch at the suggestion, but he didn't take it to heart. As tempting as the offer was, he knew Jake was only teasing. "Bullshit. One of these days you're going to catch me in the right mood and I'm going to call your bluff, buddy. Besides, didn't Logan tell you to stop harassing me at work?"

"Mm-hmm, but what Logan doesn't know won't hurt him."

"Oh, really?"

Both he and Jake jumped and swiveled around at the sound of Logan's deep voice in the doorway. Damn, the man had a bad habit of sneaking up on them. He needed a cowbell around his neck or something.

Jake scowled and rose to his feet. "As always, you have shitty timing, Logan."

Logan turned his gaze on Aaron and then pointedly looked at the clock behind him. "Shouldn't you be off, Aaron? I'm not paying you for overtime so you can hang around and flirt with my brother."

Logan's remark stung. Somebody was certainly in a crabby mood. "Yeah. Well, I was just about to lock up when Jake stopped by." He turned to Jake, standing beside him. "Sorry. Guess we'll have to pick up the rest of that conversation later. The boss man might pop a blood vessel if he has to pay me more than the minuscule amount he usually does." Logan wasn't the only one who could be an asshole when the mood suited him.

Aaron made his way to the exit. Logan's large frame halfway blocked the door, his long legs a shoulder's width apart, hands curled aggressively at his sides, but Aaron didn't let that faze him. He just skirted around the big man, careful to keep his eyes averted and not—absolutely not—touch him in any way. The last thing he needed to do was give his damn cock a reason to wake up and wave hi. Whatever had made Logan pissed had nothing to do with him, and he wanted to keep it that way.

He pulled the door shut behind him. The sound of voices rising in anger floated on the air behind him as he made his way out of the vestibule and into the summer sunshine. Things were getting way too weird in the office lately. Maybe it was a good thing he was leaving. Between Logan's surliness and Jake's flirting, he wasn't sure how much more he could stand.

Chapter Four

Thursday was nothing to write home about. The day was interminably long, with customers calling in to bitch and complain about one thing or another all day. The rain had interrupted the outside work they'd contracted, or they thought something should be fixed that wasn't. Though he had nothing to do with any of it, it was Aaron's job to try and placate each and every one of them and make sure they were satisfied by the end of the conversation.

Mark, his new sidekick, was a huge help. Having someone to talk to while Logan stormed in and out of the office, gruff to the point of being downright mad the majority of the day, helped pass the time.

Mark actually had a flair for dealing with people, which Aaron lacked. While he was quick to apologize and assure compensation, Mark talked circles around them until they probably weren't even sure why they'd called. It was only a stall tactic, because Logan would do his best to make sure each and every one of his clients walked away happy with their final product, but it took some of the pressure off the office and Aaron.

By the time he got home, it was almost six. He hurried through a quick shower and shave. Rifling from end to end inside his tiny closet for something to wear proved even harder than he had imagined. He had no idea what people wore to an art gallery or where Ross would be taking him to dinner afterward. Knowing Ross, it could be anything from the dollar menu at McDonald's to drinks and chicken wings at Hoosiers, the gay equivalent of Hooters.

He settled on khaki slacks and a navy polo. Work wear. It was semi-casual, pretty much the best he could do short of wearing the tux his mom had bought him the year before for his cousin Betsy's formal wedding. Nothing short of torture would convince him to wear that thing again.

A quick comb though his unruly red hair and he was ready. If Ross wanted someone sophisticated on his arm, he should have called another friend.

Aaron glanced at the clock on his microwave as he made his way into the miniscule kitchenette—6:35. Not bad time management there. He grabbed the green, hard plastic watering can off the floor next to his mini-fridge and set about watering his plants. He'd just finished with the last when the buzzer rang.

Showtime.

He patted his back pocket to make sure he'd remembered his wallet and strode out the door, locking it behind him. Jogging down the narrow stairs, he spotted Ross through the entrance door, tapping the toe of his Converse sneaker on the cracked cement landing. He was dressed in wrinkled black jeans and a faded Aerosmith T-shirt, his shaggy black hair sticking up in odd little spikes from all the wax he'd rubbed in it. Even with the casual attire Aaron had chosen, Ross still made him feel overdressed.

Must not be a fancy shindig after all. Good. One less thing for him to feel self-conscious about.

He pushed through the door, careful to make sure it closed completely behind him, and approached Ross. "You could have told me it was 'come as you are.' I would've worn jeans."

Ross shrugged his shoulders. "Didn't think about it. You know me, forgetful." He pretended to look Aaron over with a critical eye. "You look fine in what you have on, though," Ross said, already turning back toward where his fire-engine-red Mustang was parked at the curb.

"Yeah, I know you." Forgetful and frivolous—two words that summed Ross up well.

21

Aaron trailed after him. Not for the first time, he wondered how much his pal had sunk into restoring the classic car. He didn't know enough about vehicles to guess, but he figured it probably would've been cheaper to just buy a new one.

Ross unlocked the doors, and Aaron opened his, dropping down into the white leather bucket seat. Ross turned over the ignition and revved it up, making the engine rumble. "Sounds like a dream, doesn't she?"

"Uh, yeah, sure." It sounded loud more than anything else, but the extra vibrations felt good under his bottom. Maybe that was what Ross liked so well about it. He swallowed a snicker. "So, what time does this thing start? Eight? You never said over the phone."

"Seven." Ross dropped his hand over the eight-ball gear shifter between them on the floor and guided it into first, pulling out onto the road.

"I hate to break it to you, Ross, but it's after seven now."

Ross took his eyes off the street and shot him a condescending expression. "I know. You need to be fashionably late to these things. If you show up too early, you look like you're trying too hard, you know?"

"Oh, um, yeah. Good idea." What it sounded like was a good excuse for not being able to tell time. Who'd thought to make it a fashion statement?

Ross guided the car effortlessly through the traffic congestion as they neared the college campus. "This guy, Dalton Kenneth, who's doing the show, is so hot. You just wait until you see him. You'll melt into a puddle of goo. I've got dibs on him, though, so hands off. God, I hope he's queer. It would be such a shame to waste all that angst and raw masculinity on a breeder."

God, Ross was a drama queen. Maybe coming with him hadn't been such a good idea. Visions of standing in the corner, being ignored, filtered through his mind. He'd never made a good wingman. "Mm-hmm, a real tragedy. Good luck with the guy, and don't worry about me stepping on your toes. I'll do my best to resist, since you've got your heart set on him."

Ross made a right and steered the car into a small parking lot behind one end of short, brick strip mall. He killed the engine and they got out. While Aaron glanced around, taking in the park across the street, where children played noisily, and the quaint cobblestone walkways between each building, he heard the beep of the car alarm being set and Ross's footsteps walking around the car to join him.

"Come on, time's a-wasting."

Aaron let his friend lead the way. He knew the roundabout location of the gallery, but wasn't sure of its exact location. With little attention for art, he hadn't really cared to visit the place before it'd been closed down for remodeling over the winter.

That thought stopped him in his tracks. Remodeling. Jake and Logan had both worked on the project. They were sure to have been on the guest list. Actually, now that he thought about it, hadn't he taken a message from Jake about some kind of business gathering both brothers had to attend tonight?

Why hadn't he thought of that before?

Shit.

Several feet ahead, Ross turned to glower at him. "You coming or what?"

"Yeah…yeah, I'm coming." He jogged to catch up.

Ross led him between buildings and turned to the right, quickly making his way down the street. At the end of the block sat the art gallery, Evocative Art.

Aaron stopped to admire the display window. Three white pillars, their pedestals draped with matching swatches of black velvet, each held a sculpture. Though all clearly from different mediums—wood, some kind of metal, and clay—they all looked extraordinarily phallic in shape. On the back wall, three black and white minimalist paintings hung at strategic spots between each pillar. He had no idea what the paintings were supposed to resemble. Did that make them abstract and minimalist? Aaron shook his head as he followed Ross inside through a stained-glass door. He'd never been able to remember the appropriate names for each type of art. It was all too confusing to him.

Inside, the humid heat from outside was instantly replaced by cool, dry air. Aaron shivered at the drastic change in temperature. It was like walking out of a sauna and plunging headfirst into a refrigerator. His arms instantly rose and folded across his chest, trying to generate a little heat.

Brightly lit, the interior was a stark white. The large, open room housed a plethora of art. Sculptures rested upon raised white stands, while colorful paintings were splashed over two of the three interior walls. The back wall was empty, a single, small door in its center. Probably an entrance into storage or something. People gathered in clusters throughout the room, whispering quietly to one another. Unlike the image his mind had conjured of snobs loitering around in evening wear while waiters milled about serving hors d'oeuvres and champagne from sterling silver trays, the majority of the people looked down-to-earth and normal. The clientele seemed to range from poor college students like himself to what he thought of as professional people, older and probably moneyed, but not showy about it.

Ross tugged on Aaron's sleeve, pointing to a large group of people toward the back. "There. See the guy slumping against the wall, wearing all black. That's Dalton. Isn't he hot?"

"Mm-hmm," Aaron replied after casting a quick glance. The man was okay, but not enough to go all ga-ga over.

"I told you he was the ultimate hunk of man candy. I just love that little goatee he's sporting. It's going feel so good against my ass when he's licking my balls."

"Holy shit, Ross." Aaron cast a surreptitious look around them to see if anyone had overheard. "Watch your mouth. There are little old ladies in here. Jeez."

Before Ross abandoned him to go off in search of his latest conquest—which took all of ten seconds—Aaron scanned the room, hoping to see a familiar face. Across the way, a throng of bodies between them, he spotted not one, but two familiar figures standing side by side, head and shoulders above the crowd of art aficionados. Aaron could only make out their profiles—identical sloping foreheads, the straight bridge of two strong noses, thin lips, and equally square chins—but it was all he needed to identify them.

Now they were the epitome of the term "man candy." Separate, they were gorgeous; together, they were breathtaking. Aaron sucked in a stunned breath when an image of being plastered between them, naked and in the process of taking on both men at the same time, flittered through his imagination.

Blood rushed south, filling his cock. The thought of taking one of them in his mouth while the other fucked his ass sent a jolt of electricity through his groin. His ass clenched, the entire lower half of his body tightening.

God, why hadn't he ever fantasized about that before? For some reason, the idea had never occurred to him. There was no getting rid of it now. His cock reacted like someone had shocked him with a volt of electricity. It ached in time to his heartbeat.

Forcing his eyes away from the twins, he turned in the opposite direction from them and walked away before he was spotted. He couldn't take being around either of them tonight. Not when he was so desperate for companionship, so damn horny.

Some weird rendering of the Spanish Inquisition, done in black and red, caught his attention and he pretended to study it. Out of the corner of his eyes, he inconspicuously checked out the crowd.

He needed to get laid. He might not be able to have the man he wanted, but he wasn't going to let that stop him from picking someone up. He wasn't willing to spend another lonely night beating off and dreaming of what could never be. Tired of moping around, he decided it was high time he stopped acting like a teenager with his first crush and do something. Tonight, come hell or high water, he wasn't going home alone.

Aaron moved slowly from one painting to another, keeping his eyes open for someone of interest. Unfortunately, by the time he'd walked around the room twice, he still had yet to find anyone who wasn't part of a couple or obviously straight. Looks were deceiving, but he didn't want to embarrass himself by hitting on someone who didn't give off even a slim bit of interest.

Finding someone at the gallery was hopeless. He glanced about, looking for Ross to ask if they could split early and go somewhere more interesting. Unable to spot his friend, a glimmer of dread crept down his spine. He made a hasty retreat out of the gallery and jogged back to the spot where they'd parked. Ross's car was gone. A tiny red Honda was in its place.

Shit. Fuck. Damn.

Ross had abandoned him there in exchange for a piece of ass. The bastard could have at least said he was leaving. The worst thing was that this wasn't the first time Ross had pulled this kind of stunt. Aaron should've expected it, but hadn't, which made him feel gullible and stupid.

He slumped, his shoulders tucking inward, and walked across the darkened lot toward the park across the street. There, he chose a swing and plopped his butt down on it, toeing the pressed dirt and grass at his feet.

Dusk was giving way to night, the sun only a tiny pink crescent lingering over the horizon. Having forgotten to wear a watch, Aaron had no idea what time it was, but judging by the sun's progression, he guessed it was somewhere near nine. Summer in full swing, darkness came later and later.

His stomach growled, reminding him he hadn't eaten since lunch. In a moment, he would get up and walk home. His apartment was only about five miles away, so it wasn't that big a deal. He didn't particularly like to walk long distances at night, but the buses quit running at six, leaving him little choice. Once home, he could change into something more comfortable, eat a quick bite to tide him over, and walk down to the Irish pub two blocks from his building. It wasn't a gay bar, but a lot of students frequented it and he'd gotten lucky there a time or two before. With a little good fortune, he would run into someone compatible there again. He wouldn't know until he tried, though. Which meant he needed to get up off his ass and start the long walk home.

"Now why doesn't it surprise me that you'd prefer a playground over a perfectly good party?"

Chapter Five

Aaron jerked back, his gaze flying from his feet up to the man—Logan or Jake, though he couldn't tell which—who stood a couple of yards away. The sudden movement caused him to overbalance in the swing. The seat shot forward, while his torso went backward. His back hit the ground, startling him, but doing no real damage to anything other than his pride.

The man appeared above him, the wry twist to his sinfully shaped lips automatically identifying him as Jake. Logan was much too serious most of the time. "You okay?" He held out his hand.

"Yeah," Aaron replied as he accepted Jake's hand and allowed himself to be hauled to his feet. "Haven't I already told you to quit sneaking up on me?" Aaron wiped bits of grass off his clothes as he glared at Jake.

"Uh, no." Jake frowned. "And I didn't mean to surprise you. It's not like I was hiding in the bushes and jumped out yelling 'Boo.' Besides, you wouldn't startle so easy if you would just relax a little. You're too damn high-strung."

"Fuck you," Aaron responded defensively.

Jake chuckled, the deep, husky sound going right to Aaron's balls, the fickle bastards that they were. "About time."

"Huh?" Maybe he'd conked his head harder than he thought 'cause Aaron had no idea what Jake was talking about.

"I've been waiting for you to drop that proper little façade you wear around the office all day and be yourself. I just knew you'd be a spitfire as soon as you learned to let go a little." Jake's arm extended and his fingers brushed over the side of Aaron's face. Aaron's gaze widened at the touch. Jake shrugged. "You had a bit of grass on your cheek."

Jake's touch lingered, and Aaron had to bite down on the inside of his cheek to keep from moaning, or worse. When Jake's thumb grazed the corner of his lips, a tremor ran down Aaron's spine. Jake's scent surrounded him, wrapped him in its musky essence, a light hint of spicy cologne teasing his nose. He wanted to close his eyes and lose himself in the moment, but couldn't allow himself the pleasure. Showing his absorption in something as simple as a gentle touch would be way too telling about his feelings.

A voice in his head spoke up, warning him that it wasn't Jake he was attracted to. He was only responding so strongly because of the resemblance to Logan. Wasn't he?

"You're so beautiful."

Jake's huskily whispered words yanked Aaron out of his musings. He shook his head, his cheeks heating because of the compliment. "No, I'm not. I'm—" There was nothing special about him. He was too short, too skinny, too everything.

He couldn't do this. His dick throbbed angrily in response to his choice, but he ignored it and jerked away from Jake. Immediately, he missed the connection, but he forced himself to take an extra step back, needing more distance between them. The temptation to return the gentle touch, to see where it might lead, rode him hard. Jake's allure was almost too strong to resist, but Aaron persevered. There was no other option.

Letting go of his tightly held restraint would be akin to playing with fire. And though he knew better, his body craved the heat Jake offered. Craved it worse than a nicotine addict does a smoke right after sex.

Aaron inwardly groaned. Sex. Visions of him and Jake, their limbs sweaty and flushed by a vigorous round of fucking, popped into his head. The image was so real, he could almost feel the damp heat, taste the salty tang of well-earned perspiration. He didn't even need Jake to torment him; he was doing a good enough job of it himself.

Jake stepped forward and reached for him. Aaron hastily backpedaled away. His ass smacked into something hard and cylindrical. He felt around behind him, touched cool metal, and realized he'd run into one of the poles anchoring the swing set. He squeezed his eyes shut. Jesus, he was a klutz.

Strong hands bracketed his shoulders. "Look at me."

Aaron shook his head in answer, refusing to open his eyes. He was being childish and he knew it, but it would be all too easy to lose himself in those dark, mesmerizing eyes. Casual sex was fine, not a thing wrong with it, but he couldn't make love to Jake and not let his feelings for Logan get in the way. Jake clearly only wanted a plaything and would move on as soon as the thrill of the conquest was over. By then, it would be too late. Aaron would be head over heels and shit out of luck.

A finger caressed Aaron's jaw, tilting his chin up. "Am I that unattractive to you, Aaron?"

Aaron could hear the smile in Jake's voice, and it incensed him. The smug bastard knew full well that wasn't the problem. He opened his eyes and glowered up at Jake, who towered over him, close to six inches taller than Aaron's own five foot nine. "Stop it, Jake. Quit toying with me."

A frown creased Jake's forehead. "I'm not—" His voice cut off, and then with a little shake of his head he leaned down, bringing their eyes into alignment. The tip of his nose ran over Aaron's in feathery Eskimo kisses.

Aaron pressed his hands into Jake's chest and felt Jake's heartbeat thundering against his palms. His fingers flexed over Jake's pecs, unable to resist, and he wanted to moan in response to the wicked feel of them contracting against his touch. "I don't know what you want from me."

Okay, so that wasn't precisely the truth. It was clear enough what Jake wanted. The question resting heavy on Aaron's mind was why. In all the time he'd worked for Remora's Construction, Jake had never come on to him. Sure, they'd flirted back and forth a little bit, but that was it. Aaron couldn't understand why Jake was hitting on him now. It made no sense.

Jake quirked a single brow. "Don't you?" The pad of his thumb rubbed over Aaron's bottom lip. The short, clean nail poked into the tightly clenched crease of Aaron's mouth, applying pressure, until he gave in and parted his lips. The tip slipped inside, massaged the delicate inner lining of his lips, and moved deeper to tease the flat of his tongue.

Aaron's determination not to fool around with Jake began to crumble. His lids lowered, heavy with forbidden desire, and his lips closed over the thick digit. He pulled it deeper, applying suction, and pretended it was Jake's cock in his mouth. All he had to do was give in, and he could make that fantasy a reality.

Fuck it. He'd always been responsible, was always the first person to do the right thing in any situation. Now, just this once, he wanted to do something reckless and fun. He knew screwing around with Jake was wrong, especially since he would probably pretend he was with Logan, but couldn't help desiring anyway. As long as Jake didn't know who he was fantasizing about, what difference did it make? It was the same thing as people who closed their eyes and pretended they were fucking a movie star instead of their significant other.

Consequences be damned. He could worry about them later. Tonight, he was going to reach for the brass ring and take what was being offered to him. One night with either Remora brother would be better than a month of Sundays with anyone else.

Aaron dropped his arms to his sides, met Jake's eyes, and flicked his tongue over the thumb in his mouth. Jake's ragged inhalation in response was loud and exhilarating. Aaron's pulse pounded in his ears. His blood ran hot and went haywire as it traveled south, making him ache from long-denied need.

In the span of a single sigh, Jake closed the empty space between them. The hand cupping Aaron's jaw was joined by its mate, framing his face. Jake angled Aaron's head at precisely the right angle, popped his thumb from Aaron's mouth, and replaced it with his lips. Smooth, butter-soft lips converged on Aaron's. His eyes fell closed and he leaned into the kiss, his arms rising of their own volition to wrap around Jake's neck and urge him closer. Fully clothed, with their chests plastered together and lips locked in embrace, getting closer was an impossibility, but Aaron's lust-shrouded mind didn't comprehend that. All he knew was that he wanted more, everything Jake was willing to give.

Jake's lips parted and Aaron's followed suit. Their mouths undulated over and against one another's, soft as butterfly wings. Jake teased Aaron, flicking his tongue over and away from Aaron's mouth before he could capture it and suck on it, the way he wanted. Aggravation ran rampant, firing his blood, making him desperate for a better, deeper taste of Jake.

A smile tugged at the corner of his lips as he let go of Jake's nape and reached down to palm the impressive bulge that strained against the fly of Jake's slacks. Hot and hard, the ridge of Jake's dick twitched as if trying to jump through the slick fabric of its prison and into Aaron's hand.

Jake's hips thrust forward, pressing into Aaron's touch at the same time his lips ran a trail of drugging kisses down the side of the Aaron's throat. Aaron groaned and arched his neck, making extra room for Jake to continue. Jake's mouth felt so good on his skin. He wanted it to stop, to progress, to never end. He didn't know what he wanted. Just more.

Blunt teeth nipped at Aaron's ear. A hand snuck around his waist and squeezed the side of one ass cheek. While a moist tongue laved his earlobe, soothing away the sting, Aaron released his hold on Jake's cock, both hands zeroing in on the tightest ass he'd ever felt. His dick jerked and his hips lurched forward, grinding against Jake's pelvis. The other man's desire was clear. Aaron felt it pressing back against him, even through all the layers of clothing between them. Clothing that suddenly seemed too restrictive, damn near suffocating.

The clothes had to go. One hand still on Jake's ass, Aaron squeezed the other between them and located Jake's zipper. Trembling fingers latched onto the tab and tugged down, intent on wrapping around the sweet prick waiting below. He needed to see it, touch and taste, before he imploded.

Jake's mouth stilled on the curve of Aaron's throat. Hot breath beat against the joint of his neck and shoulder as the tips of his fingers parted the soft fabric of Jake's slacks and slipped inside. Hot, hair-roughened skin met his fingertips. Holy God, no underwear. He bent his wrist, delved a little deeper to the left, and discovered what he sought. His world narrowed and centered on the long, hard cock within his reach. He brushed over the tip, elated when he felt the abundance of silky moisture that gave away Jake's desire for him. He petted the widely flared crown and shallow dip beneath, concentrating on what he could reach.

He must have been doing something right, because Jake's cock quivered and the man let out a shaky groan. He lifted his head, rained kisses up the side of Aaron's jaw to his mouth, and kissed him. Their lips danced together, increasing in intensity with every pass. Jake nipped at Aaron's lower lip. His tongue swept over it and delved past, into the interior of Aaron's mouth. The sugary taste of butterscotch candy and a hint of something richer, the intrinsic flavor all Jake's own, burst over Aaron's taste buds, more intoxicating than liquor. He moaned and kissed Jake back, their tongues slip-sliding over and under each other.

Aaron tightened his hand around Jake's cock, compressing the damp, spongy tip. It flexed and twitched in his grip. Jake gasped and shook, breaking their kiss. He batted Aaron's hand away from his groin and rested his forehead against the top of Aaron's head. "Jesus. Being with you is going to give me a heart attack."

Aaron laughed, a bit of his reservations draining away. "You'll be all right," he whispered, fingering the slit in Jake's cockhead. "I promise not to be too rough on you, old man."

"Smartass," Jake replied, pressing their lips back together again and plunging his tongue into Aaron's mouth.

The words set off a twinge of déjà vu that nagged just out of reach at the back of Aaron's consciousness. He shoved it down and let himself be swept away by the hard cock in his hand and the flexible tongue in his mouth. Everything about Jake was seductive and…right. Was it possible that he'd had feelings for Jake all this time and not been aware of them?

Jake fumbled with Aaron's zipper, sliding it down with ease, and Aaron decided he could worry about messy emotional shit later. Jake's hand slipped inside his fly and wiggled through the slot in his cotton boxers, gripping Aaron's cock in

32

a firm, callused fist. Aaron's thoughts scattered into a million pieces. The only thing left was pure sensation, Jake's breath filling his lungs as they kissed, Jake's hand stroking his cock with long, hard pulls, Jake all around him. When Jake's free hand slid under Aaron's shirt and found his nipple, pinching it, he lost any control he had over his body.

Every muscle locked up, his ass clenching, as wave upon wave of liquid lightning poured out of his cock and into Jake's fist. He cried out in Jake's mouth, unable to stay silent. Jake swallowed it down, his hand still loosely pumping Aaron's waning erection in an attempt to drain Aaron's balls of every drop.

Through it all, Jake kissed and petted him, keeping Aaron upright between his huge body and the steel pole at Aaron's back while he shook and shivered, his legs too unsteady to hold him up. As the mind-numbing orgasm calmed, he was surprised to feel Jake's hard cock still in his hand. Adrift in his own pleasure, he'd forgotten to see to his lover's. That wouldn't do at all.

He pressed a hard, closed-lip kiss to Jake's mouth and dropped to his knees. His hands trembling, he pulled opened Jake's pants and jerked them down. Jake's penis sprang up though the parted folds of black cotton fabric, long and thick. Aaron tugged until the slacks were halfway down Jake's muscular thighs. There he stopped, in awe of Jake's masculinity.

A light dusting of silky dark hair surrounded the root of a fat, uncut cock and full, round balls. His fingers trailed over the wrinkled sac while his eyes feasted on the moist, weeping head of Jake's cock. Having never seen one before, Aaron was fascinated by Jake's foreskin, pulled back tight around the wide flare of his cockhead. He couldn't resist leaning forward and swiping the damp tip with the flat of his tongue. He moaned, reveling in the bittersweet taste bursting over his palate.

A hand carded through his hair, gently petting. "Please," Jake whispered into the night. "Suck me. Make me come."

Aaron's pulse soared, exhilarated that he could make such a strong man want him so bad. He sucked the tip into his mouth, twisted his tongue over and around the head, tasting and teasing. He glanced up at Jake, looming over him, and saw the big man staring down at him, watching his every move with dark, hungry eyes.

Aaron cupped Jake's balls, rolling them in his palms as he spread his jaw wide and sucked more cock into his mouth. He caressed it with lips, tongue, and palate, Hoovering it in and out, while the hand around the base pumped in rhythm with his mouth.

Every one of his senses seemed heightened. He felt lost in the moment, in tune with the man beside him to the exception of all else. The strong, slightly musky smell of Jake's desire. The feel of soft skin and hard muscle sliding in and out of his mouth, butting into the back of his throat. The cool night air wafting over his face, while Jake's hand caressed his cheek, silently urging him on.

Aaron tightened his lips around Jake's cock and sucked hard, desperate to make him come, to feel his seed splashing over his tongue and down the back of his throat. He gently squeezed and manipulated Jake's heavy balls, pressing the knuckle of his pointer against the thin strip of silky skin.

Jake groaned, long and low. His body stiffened. "Aaron… Gonna come. Oh. Gonna…"

Aaron felt the swollen crown of Jake's cock throb under his tongue a split second before salty, tart jets of come began to fill his mouth. He swallowed, gentling his suction, while he continued to bathe Jake's cockhead with his tongue.

Jake shivered, the tremor passing down through his large frame. His dress pants, precariously hanging around his thighs, slipped and fell to his knees. Aaron released Jake's softening penis, almost reluctant to release it, and noticed that Jake's wallet had dropped out of his pocket.

Jake caught Aaron's chin and tilted it up. Bending at the waist, he leaned down and kissed him. "Thank you. You're damn good at that."

Aaron blushed. "You're welcome." It wasn't as if he'd never heard that before, but Jake sounded so sincere about it. His praise was flattering.

34

"You dropped your wallet." Aaron licked his lips, still tasting Jake, and stretched forward to grab it. The wallet was the small, black leather fold-over type, the kind men carried in their back pocket. He picked it up off the ground, and when he did, it flipped open, revealing a line of cards on one side and a plastic-covered ID slot on the other. He glanced down at it, interested to see how horrible Jake's mug shot from the DMV was, and felt a tight, empty knot form in the pit of his stomach. The blood drained from his face, making him nauseous and dizzy. Jake's name wasn't on the license; Logan's was.

He scrambled backward, the steel pole biting into his back. He pulled up his zipper, wincing at the icky wet feeling inside his pants, and rose to his feet, the wallet held out in front of him between two fingers, as if it were contaminated with toxic waste. "Jake?" He wouldn't jump to conclusions. He wouldn't. "Um, why do you have Logan's wallet?"

Jake—*please, God, let it be Jake*—took it and reached down to pull up his pants, refusing to look at Aaron. "I can explain that."

Aaron cleared his throat, too impatient to wait while his lover pulled himself together, to hear what explanation the man had to share. "Well, Jake, why do you have his wallet?"

His pants around his thighs, Jake glanced up at him. "I really wish you'd quit calling me Jake."

Aaron gasped, tried to take a step back, and plunked his head into the pole behind him. The man in front of him was Logan. His straight and married boss. Aaron cursed, barely feeling the sting to the back of his head, and tried to take a step to the side.

Jake—*no, Logan!*—let go of his pants and reached out to stop him, grabbed Aaron's arm. "Wait, Aaron, let me explain."

Aaron shook his head. He yanked his arm, putting all his weight behind it, and succeeded in getting loose. Logan was not so lucky. Aaron's vicious tug threw him off balance, his arms pin-wheeled for a single second, and then he tottered backwards, cursing as his ass hit the damp grass.

Aaron didn't wait for an explanation. He couldn't. What was the point? It didn't take a genius to figure out what had

35

just happened. Plenty of seemingly straight men played a little on the side with gay men. They used gay men like a temporary service. Wife not around? Find a gay man to blow you.

Yes, he liked to suck cock. A lot of people did. That did not mean, however, he didn't have scruples about who he blew. The funny thing was that being with Logan should have been the fruition of every wet dream he'd had in the last four years. Instead, all he felt was dirty and used. Cheap.

Hysterical laughter bubbled up in Aaron's chest as he turned and ran. The sound of Logan calling after him, pleading with him to stop, rang in his ears long after he ran the five miles home and collapsed into a nasty ball of emotion inside his front door.

Chapter Six

The sun rose on Friday morning, just like it did every day. The only difference was what it cast its cheerful rays upon. Instead of finding Aaron up and bustling around his apartment as he got ready for work, the sun found him huddled on his futon, knees hugging his chest.

The night before had been both a dream come true and a nightmare. What little sleep he'd gotten after shucking out of his soggy clothes and falling into bed was restless and plagued by lurid images of Logan fucking his mouth while the man's blonde harpy of a wife stood over Aaron's shoulder and instructed him on how to do it right. Needless to say, he didn't get much rest.

His gaze wandered to the cell phone sitting beside him on the end table. He picked it up, looked at the clock for the umpteenth time, and set it back down. He needed to piss. That needed to be taken care of first. Afterward, he would call in to work. Procrastination was a beautiful thing.

Aaron unfolded stiff limbs, his muscles having long since locked up from sitting in the same position for too long, and dragged his lethargic body up off the futon. He shuffled across the room and into the miniscule bathroom, flipping on the light as he entered. The bare bulb overhead flashed to life and momentarily blinded him. He blinked repeatedly, trying to adapt his eyesight as he made his way to the toilet and drained his bladder.

Finished, he gave his dick a shake and turned to wash his hands. The sight greeting him in the mirror wasn't a pretty one. Puffy, red-rimmed green eyes stared back at him accusingly. His hair stood up in wild disarray, some of it matted to his head, while other errant, curly red patches looked like someone had taken a teasing brush to them and forgotten to straighten out the tangles. His gaze dropped to his hands and stayed there as he soaped up and rinsed them.

As if it were a homing beacon, his gaze immediately fell on his cell phone upon exiting the bathroom. He dragged his feet on the way over to it, putting it off as long as he could. Nearing on eight, it was now or never. Though it scarcely mattered, he couldn't fathom not making the call to let Mark know he was on his own for the day. Mark had already proven he was an efficient taskmaster and could run things without Aaron's guidance. And Logan would know good and well why he wasn't there. Just because the man was a two-timing cheat didn't mean he was an idiot.

Himself, on the other hand, he wasn't so sure about. Adulterer, coward, and naïve dumb ass seemed to fit him pretty well this morning. Those same words ran on a constant loop through Aaron's mind while he picked up his cell phone and dialed the number for the office. As it rang, he prayed he'd called early enough that Logan wouldn't yet be in the office.

"Remora's Construction, Mark speaking."

Thank God. "Mark, this is Aaron."

"Oh, hey, Aaron. Uh, shouldn't you be here by now? It's almost eight."

Aaron took a deep breath. "Yeah, about that…I'm not feeling so well this morning. I think I'm coming down with a touch of the flu or something." He summoned up his best fake cough, but it came out weak and pitiful sounding. "I won't be able to make it in to work today." By the time he finished, his heart pounded a mile a minute and his palms were so slick he could barely hold on to the phone. He'd never been a good liar. Even over the phone, he sucked at it.

"Oh, that's too bad. Wasn't today supposed to be your last day, though?"

"Yeah."

"Oh, well, I hope you feel better then, and good luck with your—" Mark's voice cut off, as if he'd placed his hand over the phone, and his voice was muffled as he spoke to someone else.

Logan must have come in. Aaron quickly hung up the phone. He hit the power button and watched the screen go blank before laying it on the end table, valiantly trying to ignore the way his hand trembled.

Pussy, his inner voice chided. Maybe so, he argued, but if burying his head in the sand helped save his sanity, he was all for it.

* * * * *

The weekend was spent sequestered in his apartment.

By Monday, Aaron was a basket case. Every time he turned his phone on, it rang. After endless hounding repetitions of his frog ringtone and the vibrating buzz of voicemail notification, he'd turned the phone off and kept it that way. He didn't want to talk to anyone anyway. The urge to check his messages was tempting, but he refused to give in to curiosity. He had no interest in talking to either of the two people most likely to call him.

Running on only a handful of hours' worth of sleep in the last four days, he wasn't even close to being prepared for his first day of work at Lowe's. Since beggars couldn't be choosers, he dragged ass through the routine of getting ready for work. He needed the money too badly to blow it off just because he'd rather stay home and feel sorry for himself. Self-pity would not pay the rent, no matter how much he wanted it to.

After shaving, showering, and getting dressed, Aaron locked and left his apartment. Since Lowe's was on the other side of town, he had to leave an hour early. The bus ride across town was notoriously slow, and he didn't want to be late.

Since the bus was almost empty, he got to work with half an hour to spare. He went inside anyway, instead of loitering around outside until it was closer to the time he was supposed to arrive. Inside, the store was already abuzz with activity. People shoved oversized buggies between aisles, and employees, identifiable by the red smocks they wore, hurried about restocking shelves and waiting on customers.

He worked his way to the back of the building and walked through a set of swinging gray doors that led to the employees-only area, where the general manager's office was located. Not in his best form that morning, he hoped being early would earn him a few brownie points.

Stopping outside the first door to his left, Aaron raised his hand and knocked. A loud voice bellowed, "Come in," and he pulled the door open and stepped inside. "Good morning, Mr. Reynolds."

Sitting behind an archaic metal desk, his new boss frowned up at him. "To you, too, Mr. Samuels, but I'm not sure what you're doing here. Didn't you get my message?"

Aaron grimaced. Damn, what a shitty time to decide not to answer the blasted phone. "No, sir. I'm sorry, but my cell's been on the fritz for the past couple of days."

The man scratched his bald head and nodded. "Well, I'm sorry to have to tell you this, son, but we offered you the position on the contingency of your references checking out. When my assistant called your previous office, he was told that you quit without notice."

"But I didn't—" Aaron began to sputter before Mr. Reynolds held up a hand, shushing him.

"I'm sorry, son. In this business, we're only as good as our help, and I have to be able to depend on my management being reliable."

Aaron floundered for something, anything, he could say to make this right. He couldn't tell the man the truth, and nothing else came to mind that wouldn't make him sound like a belligerent child.

The phone rang, and his opportunity to save his ass was gone. Mr. Reynolds tipped his head toward the phone, compassion in his beady gray eyes. "I need to take this. Best of luck to you in your job search, Mr. Samuels." He picked up the phone and turned his back on Aaron, dismissing him.

Aaron walked out of Lowe's in a fog. He couldn't believe Logan would be vindictive enough to give him a bad reference. How could he be such a poor judge of character? The pedestal he'd kept Logan on, still whole even after Thursday's fallout, went up in a fiery ball of smoke.

He had no job and no prospects. With less than fifty bucks in his checking account, it wouldn't be long before he was flat broke and out of luck. No reference for the last four years meant he'd be lucky to get a job flipping burgers.

In a nutshell, he was screwed.

Absorbed by his thoughts, Aaron stepped off the curb in front of the store without watching where he was going. A horn sounded just as the chrome grill of a truck jumped into his peripheral vision. He slapped the hood, pissed off at the world in general, and looked up to give the careless fucking driver a piece of his mind.

Aaron sucked in his breath. Logan. Their eyes met through the windshield of the crew cab truck and clashed. Why was the bastard here? Had he came to gloat about his misdeeds?

Logan had the audacity to smile at him over the steering wheel. A red haze clouded Aaron's vision. He stalked around the side of the cab, his muscles tensing up and his hands balling into fists at his sides.

Logan opened the door and slipped out, slamming the door closed behind him. "Hey, Aaron, I've been trying to get a hold of you "

He clenched his fingers, pulled back his arm, and punched Logan square in the nose. Logan's head popped backward and hit the truck. A hand flew to his nose, his spread fingers spanning outward over the lower half of his face.

Aaron stepped back and tried to shake the sting out of his knuckles. Though shocked he'd actually hit someone, part of Aaron was proud for having done it. He'd never stood up to anyone in his life, not physically, and the way he figured it, his timing couldn't have been better. Someone needed to hit the jackass. He had as much right to do the honors as anyone else.

His satisfaction was short-lived. Logan dropped the hand covering his face, revealing a dull red nose and a snarling upper lip. He advanced on Aaron and grabbed him by the shoulders, spinning him around until his back was pressed into the hot metal and cool glass of the truck door. Aaron struggled against the hand Logan pressed into the middle of his chest, but it wouldn't budge. Finally, he quit wiggling and stared up at Logan, waiting to see what he'd do next.

"What in the hell is your problem? First, you run off on me Thursday. Then you bail on me Friday. Now you're throwing punches? Are you on something? This isn't like you, Aaron."

"Fuck you, Logan. You know exactly why I punched you. Don't even try to pretend you don't." Aaron attempted to jerk away again, only to end up plunking his head back into the glass. That only served to piss him off more. "Let me the fuck go, or I'll tell your wife exactly what you were doing to me on Thursday." The threat may not have been the best course to take, judging by the way Logan's face drained of color. Not that he had any intention of doing it. The woman deserved to know what her scumbag husband was doing behind her back, but he wasn't going to be the one to do it. Let someone else break the news to the little missus. He just wanted to forget the whole thing. Which was easier said than done with more than six feet of angry man towering over him, ready to tear him a new asshole.

"Is that what this is about?"

Aaron sneered. "Ding, ding, ding, we have a winner. You finally figured it out, did you? Good for you. Now, let go of me."

The hand digging into his breastbone dropped away, and Aaron heaved a sigh of relief. With Logan pressing a considerable amount of his weight into his chest, it had been a little hard to breathe. He would have rather suffocated than admit it, though.

Logan took a half step back but put his hands on the truck to either side of Aaron, pinning him in. "We need to talk."

Aaron ducked under Logan's arm on the side not hampered by the rearview mirror. Sometimes being short had its advantages. "No, we don't. I have nothing to say to you."

Aaron only made it two steps before Logan's paw wrapped around his biceps and jerked him to a halt. "You may not have anything to say to me, but I have some things to say to you."

"I don't give a flyin' "

Logan hunched down until they were eye to eye. "You're going to hear me out, and that's final." He shoved his shoulder into Aaron's middle and lifted him up off his feet.

"Put me down, damn it!" Aaron screeched as he was lugged up and over Logan's shoulder. As the man carried him around to the passenger side door, Aaron stared down at the fine ass he'd spent years daydreaming about and magically didn't think about fucking it. All he wanted to do now was kick it into next week. "Who the fuck do you think you are? Put me down!" He punctuated his demand with a wiggle and a kick to the front of Logan's body. He couldn't tell what he'd hit, but Logan grunted at the impact. That was good enough for him, so he did it again.

In retaliation, the flat of Logan's huge hand crashed down on his ass, stinging like fire. "Ouch. Fuck!"

Logan pulled open the passenger door. "That's what you get for kicking me in the gut, you little shit."

"Put me down like I asked, and I wouldn't have had to kick you, asshole."

"Your wish is my command." Logan unceremoniously dumped him onto the bench seat, slammed the door closed, and started around the front of the cab.

Aaron immediately reached for the handle and tugged. Nothing. He would've tried the window, but the controls were electric and there was no chance he could break it before Logan got in. "Fuck."

42

Logan slipped behind the wheel. "Thought you might try that. Child safety locks are a beautiful thing."

Aaron slumped back against the seat and glared at Logan. "Bastard."

Chapter Seven

Silence stretched like a yawning void between Aaron and Logan as the truck's wheels ate into the pavement. Staring sullenly out the window, Aaron wore what felt like a permanent scowl on his face. With every few miles that passed between Lowe's and wherever the hell Logan was taking him, he shot wayward glances at Logan. Each time he would open his mouth, ready to demand Logan stop the truck and let him out, only to go back to silently staring out the window. Though he was ashamed that he cared, he was curious to find out what Logan had to say. Not that he would ever admit it.

When Logan bypassed the off-ramp leading toward the office and instead turned off the highway at an unfamiliar exit, a hint of unease wiggled into his gut and wouldn't abate. It didn't lessen until Logan pulled off the main road through a copse of trees and started up a long gravel driveway that led to a secluded log cabin.

The house wasn't Aaron's idea of what a cabin in the woods should look like. Nothing about it was small or quaint. Huge, reflective windows peeked out of the redwood siding, dominating the front of the house. The goliath cabin stood tall and proud, amid a backdrop of wild foliage and tall oaks standing like sentinels in the background.

Logan pulled the truck to a stop next to the house and turned off the engine. Silence reigned for a moment, neither of them speaking. Aaron glanced at Logan out of the corner of his eye, waiting.

Finally, Logan broke the quiet. "Are you going to come in under your own free will, or am I going to have to throw you over my shoulder again? I ask because you aren't as light as you look, and I'd rather not give myself a hernia if I can help it."

Aaron snorted and suppressed the grin trying to crawl over his face. "It would serve you right for acting like a fucking caveman."

Logan chuckled. "Maybe so. Well, what's it going to be, walk or ride?"

The smile withered and died when something else occurred to Aaron. He twisted around in his seat and faced Logan, wanting to read the man's face as he spoke. "What about your wife? I don't feel comfortable going into the home you share with her after everything that's happened."

Logan looked directly into Aaron's eyes. "You don't need to worry about her. We need to talk about that and a lot of other things, but I don't want to do it sitting out here in the truck. Come inside with me and I'll explain everything, I promise."

"Okay," Aaron whispered, wondering if he would regret taking Logan at his word.

They got out of the truck, and Aaron followed Logan up to the door, waiting outside while Logan punched numbers into a keypad to turn off the security alarm. Finished, Logan waved him in, and Aaron trailed after him. Nervous and expecting to be ambushed by a pissed-off spouse at any moment, Aaron followed him through the house.

Logan guided him through an open foyer, the walls white and the hardwood flooring beneath their feet stained to a deep cherry. Aaron tried to keep one eye on Logan ahead of him, while scanning his surroundings at the same time. He caught quick glimpses into a lower-level living room, decorated in shades of blue and cream, and what looked like a wood-paneled office with rows of bookshelves. Finally, they rounded a corner at the end of the hall and stepped into a large, airy eat-in kitchen. One end of the huge room was fashioned into a dining room of sorts, including a table long enough to fit a small army and a hutch filled with china. On the other end of the room were the appliances and double sink   all gleaming chrome finishes   and a long countertop fashioned out of beige-and-gray, swirled marble between the stove and fridge. Everything was spotless and harmonious in its symmetry. Small details here and there caught his eye the most. Small, potted herb plants sitting on the windowsill behind the sink, a white lace runner on the dining table, even the delicate china shelved in the hutch. All were little things that spoke of a woman's touch more than the gruff man he'd come to know. A realization which made him slightly queasy.

His gaze drifted to Logan, who stood regarding Aaron with the same intensity Aaron had been paying to his house. "So," Logan said as he pulled out a chair at the table and sat, waving to the one beside it for Aaron, "What do you think?"

That I want to puke. "Nice house. Your wife has good taste." The last bit came out a little more snarky than he'd intended, but he couldn't very well call it back now that it hung out in the air between them. Frankly, he wasn't sure he would have even if he had the option. Better to get this unpleasantness finished quickly so he could get back to trying to figure out what he was going to do with his life now that he'd hit rock bottom.

Logan laughed. "I decorated the house, Aaron, but thanks anyway." He nudged the chair beside him with the toe of his boot. "Have a seat."

Aaron crossed his arms over his chest. "I'll stand."

Logan shrugged and sat back. "Suit yourself."

When nothing more was said for several terse moments, Aaron gave in and plopped down in the chair. He glared at Logan. "Fine, I'm sitting. Now talk."

Logan scooted his chair up to the table and leaned forward on his elbows, narrowing the distance between them. "First of all, I'm not married."

Aaron rolled his eyes. "Uh-huh. And if I were naïve enough to believe that, I'm sure you've got a real nifty bridge to sell me too."

Logan tried to lay his hand over Aaron's, but Aaron jerked away at the last minute. "I'm telling you the truth."

He pointedly glanced down at the gold band on Logan's left hand, where it rested on the table. "And the wedding ring?"

"It's a reminder never to let myself be forced into something I don't want."

"Uh-huh."

"What do you want me to do, dig up my divorce papers? Call my ex and have her spell everything out to you?"

"I don't know. Just prove it. If you can…"

Logan ran a hand over his stubbly head. "How?"

"Don't care."

Logan sighed and pushed away from the table. "All right. Sit tight and I'll be back in a second."

Aaron fidgeted in his seat. In a matter of minutes, Logan walked back into the kitchen with a file folder. He set it on the table in front of Aaron. "Here. These should tell you what you want to know. Elaine and I haven't been together in over a year. The divorce was final two months ago."

Aaron picked up the folder and flipped through the thick stack of pages inside. He didn't understand half the legal jargon, but it was easy enough to get the gist of it. Logan was telling the truth. His divorce was final on the last day of April. The papers were even notarized, alleviating any worry about them being faked. Not that he thought Logan would go to that much effort anyway. Not for him. He set the folder down and slid it across the table. "Okay."

"That's it? Okay? That's all you have to say?"

"What do you expect, a pat on the back for not being an adulterous creep? It's a relief to know you aren't married, but that doesn't explain why you pretended to be Jake. Or why you gave me a bad reference and kept me from getting the job I worked damn hard to get."

"You can do better than that crappy job at Lowe's. I couldn't let you accept that position when I knew there was a better one waiting for you."

"And I suppose working for you is what you consider better?" Aaron interrupted.

"No. Someone from Annie's Nursery called Friday, wanting a reference for you. After the glowing recommendation I gave you, there's no way they won't offer you a position. I know you'd rather work in a greenhouse than that stuffy-ass home improvement store. Which I would have told you Friday had you come into work or answered your damn phone. I even tried to find your address so I could track you down at your place, but you never updated your information after you moved. I had no way to find you except to come to Lowe's and hope I would run into you there."

Aaron's anger drained away faster than water through spread fingers. "Annie's Nursery called? Really?"

"Really."

"Shit, that's great. I was wondering what I was going to do, you know, after I didn't get the job at Lowe's. I was a little scared I would end up on the streets, washing windshields to make the rent." Aaron winced. Diarrhea mouth strikes again.

"I wouldn't have let that happen, Aaron. You could have always come back to the office and worked for me. I'm going to miss not seeing your frizzy red head behind the desk every morning."

"My hair is not frizzy." It was just a little…wild some mornings.

Logan held his hands up. "Hey, if you say so, but I think it's cute."

"I am not cute." Cute was for babies and ducklings.

"You're right. You're not cute."

"Thank you." I think.

"You're beautiful. I meant it when I said it Thursday and I do now."

Aaron blushed.

"All that pale, creamy skin and your expressive green eyes. Everything you feel is transmitted right through them. I can usually tell what mood you're in just by looking at you. And then, of course, there's your tight little ass. I'm definitely going to miss seeing that rump sashay around the office."

"Yeah, right. My ass is as scrawny as the rest of me."

47

Logan's nostrils flared, and the smoldering look behind his dark, sexy eyes kicked up a notch. "No, it's not. Believe me, I had my hands all over your ass Thursday night, and there isn't anything scrawny about it."

Which brought another question to the forefront of Aaron's mind. "Why?"

Logan chuckled. "Why don't I think your ass is scrawny?"

"No. Why did you pretend to be Jake?"

The expression on Logan's face contorted, going from goofy to serious in the space of a blink. He released a long sigh and began, "I never said I was Jake. You just assumed I was."

"You could have corrected me easily enough," Aaron interrupted.

"I know. I should have said something. I started to, but then I considered the way you always tense up around me. You don't do that with Jake. It's like you're scared of me or something. I hated it, but I didn't know how to fix it. I let you believe I was Jake because it was easier to get what I wanted, to be closer to you, and for that I apologize. My only excuse is that I'd been trying to get your attention forever and you never seemed to notice. You would flirt with Jake and I..." His gaze dropped to his hands and his voice dropped a decibel. "I was jealous."

"Excuse me?" Aaron's jaw felt like it wanted to unhinge. Through force of will alone, he managed to keep his mouth closed, but it was a close call. Logan was attracted to him? And jealous because he flirted with Jake? Bullshit. He glanced over his shoulder, convinced he was on Candid Camera or something similar. Things like this just didn't happen to people like him.

Logan glanced up. "I said I was jealous. It pissed me off that you would flirt with Jake and then clam up when I tried to talk to you. I couldn't figure out how you could be attracted to him and not me, when we look exactly the same."

Laughter bubbled up in Aaron's chest and spilled out of his mouth. Once he started laughing, he couldn't stop. It was so ridiculous. All this time he'd been pining away for Logan, and the man was actually attracted to him. It was un-fucking-believable.

"I'm glad you find my discomfort so amusing."

"Oh, poor baby," Aaron replied between guffaws. "That's what you get for trying to fuck with my head."

Chapter Eight

Distracted by his mirth over how pitiful they were, both of them mooning over one another for the last year, Aaron failed to notice Logan. Strong hands latched on to him beneath his armpits and hauled him up out of his chair. Logan swept him up off his feet and plunked him down on the table, with seemingly no effort at all. Jesus, he's strong.

As he was about to object to being manhandled yet again, Aaron's complaint was swallowed by Logan's hard lips crashing over his own. Logan growled and ground their lips together, moving with a bold purpose that was neither tender nor sweet, but a desperate claiming from a man too long denied.

It was exactly what Aaron needed to let go of his reservations.

Aaron spread his legs and wound his arms around Logan's neck, pulling him into the cradle of his thighs. He buried his fingers in the coarse hair budding at Logan's nape and kissed his lover back.

The blowjob on Thursday had been great—mind-blowing, if he was honest—but at the time, he hadn't even known it was Logan. Hadn't had the chance to savor who he held in his arms or made love to with his mouth. This moment, being together in the bright kitchen and pawing at each other with a desperation neither could control, would be the moment he remembered as their first true time together. And this time, Aaron intended to get more than a hasty blowjob. He wanted to peel Logan's clothes off and lick every inch of his body, suck the long, hard cock he could feel rubbing up against his abs, and then impale himself on Logan's dick and ride him into oblivion. Anything less wouldn't suffice.

Logan teasingly rimmed the surface of Aaron's lips with his tongue. Aaron's fingers tightened around Logan's nape, and he tilted his head to the side, parting his lips as he moved. On the next pass of Logan's tongue over his bottom lip, Aaron licked back, demanding more. The time for teasing was long past.

Over, under, and around, their tongues glided together and apart. Their lips clung, moist and supple, as they ate at each other's mouths.

After what felt like an eternity and yet no time at all, Logan pulled away, his forehead dropping to Aaron's shoulder as he drew in ragged gulps of air. Aaron's own breathing was choppy at best, but he didn't let that deter him from warm bronze patch of skin directly in line with his mouth. He flicked the tip of his tongue over the galloping pulse at the base of Logan's throat, tasted salt and skin. He dove in for more, laving every available inch of skin he could find between Logan's ear and the collar of his T-shirt.

Between them, his left hand zeroed in on the expanding bulge behind Logan's fly and rubbed. His lover's hips canted forward, pressing into his touch. Aaron took that as permission and yanked at the metal button standing between him and heaven. A whimper of frustration built in the back of his throat when the damn thing wouldn't budge.

He was about to start cussing when Logan's hand gripped his wrist. Aaron looked up into deep brown eyes, gone even darker with passion. "Wait," Logan said. "I need to tell you something first."

Aaron shook his head. "Whatever it is can wait until afterward. I need you to fuck me. Right now. Please. I need you, Logan." And he was afraid to hear any more revelations this morning. What he'd already been told was more than enough. Yes, he was being a pussy, but said pussy was about to get fucked by the man he'd been in love with for almost four years, and he didn't want to take a chance on anything screwing that up.

Logan stared down at him, clearly torn. "Okay." He brushed his lips over Aaron's, soft and gentle. "We'll talk after."

Aaron was glad Logan agreed so easily. If he had to have another bomb dropped on him today, he'd much rather hear it after he was spent and boneless, not when he was so horny he could barely focus his eyes.

Impatient to get the show on the road, Aaron gave a tug to one of the loops of Logan's jeans. "You have on way too many clothes. How about taking these off for me?"

"That can be arranged, but what are you going to do for me?"

Aaron leaned back on his elbows and grinned. "Watch."

A ducky hint of rose crept up Logan's neck and splashed color over his sharp cheekbones. Considering he'd never seen the man blush, Aaron found it adorable. He made a mental note to explore Logan's fetish for being watched in the future. Right now, he was too busy watching Logan himself.

The man in question gripped the hem of his shirt and pulling it up over his head, revealing dusky copper nipples atop firm pecs, and washboard abs that flexed and rippled as he flung the shirt away from him and reached for the closure of his jeans. Aaron bit into his lip, waiting to see the pretty, uncut prick he knew hid underneath the denim pop free. When Logan's fingers didn't move, he glanced up. "Well? Get on with it."

Logan smirked. "It's your turn. Lose the shirt, baby. I didn't get to see near enough of your sexy body the other night."

Aaron flushed, but moved to do what his man desired. His man. Damn if he didn't like the sound of that. What else could he do when he was half a heartbeat away from expiring of want? He sat up, jerked his shirt out of pants, and yanked it over his head, before leaning back on his elbows. "Done. Now lose the jeans."

Logan popped the button on his jeans. "Bossy little thing, aren't you?" He lowered the zipper a millimeter at a time until a broad V of tanned skin smattered with silky black hair ap-

51

peared between the open flaps of denim. Pausing, he smiled and then shimmied the jeans down his trim hips and kicked out of them.

Sucking on his bottom lip, Aaron stared. Completely naked, Logan's body was a thing of beauty, all tanned skin and lean sinew. Wide shoulders narrowed in the classic V line to trim hips and thick thighs, heavily roped with muscle. A light dusting of black covered his arms and legs. Silky-looking hair spread between his hard pecs and thinned out into a fine line that bisected his flat abs and bloomed once again around the impressive package between his legs. Never one to like hairy men, Aaron found it strongly appealing on Logan. Everything about him screamed, manly. No one would ever mistake Logan for a teenager, like people tended to do with Aaron.

Logan pulled a chair up to the table right in front of where Aaron lay. He sat, scooting the chair up, as if he were ready to sit there and eat dinner. The thought conjured all kinds of images in Aaron's head that turned his breath and pulled his balls tight. Logan's hand crept up Aaron's thighs, the thumbs from both hands skimming over the bulge at his crotch, before reaching for the closure of his pants. "It's your turn again."

Logan deftly unbuttoned Aaron's pants and slid them down over his legs, leaving Aaron in a pair of snug navy-blue boxer-briefs that did nothing to hide his excitement. Aaron reclined and studied Logan as the man's gaze crawled over his body, praying like hell that Logan liked what he saw. Aaron wasn't ashamed of his body—his was lean and toned, well-proportioned for his smaller stature—but compared to what Logan saw in the mirror every morning, he had to appear somewhat pale and skinny.

Logan ran his hands over Aaron's chest, tweaked his nipples, and caressed the quivering skin of his abdomen. He rubbed his cheek against the cotton of Aaron's boxers and inhaled. "Damn, you smell good."

If actions spoke louder than words, Logan's told Aaron all he needed to know.

Aaron reached down and feathered his fingers over the stiff stubble on Logan's head. He'd always wondered how that short buzz cut would feel against his thighs. Now it appeared he was going to get the chance to find out.

Logan slid his fingers up the inside of Aaron's shorts and grasped the fabric, pulling it down a little at a time. His warm lips kissed every inch of skin he uncovered.

By the time Logan worked the clingy cotton over Aaron's hips, Aaron was wild with need. He shifted restlessly. Goose-bumps popped up along his limbs and torso. Fine beads of sweat appeared on his brow. "Logan, please."

Logan grinned up at him, the look on his face one of pure devilment. "Patience, baby. I need to love on you a little first."

He laved a warm, wet trail up the inside of Aaron's thigh, stopping just short of Aaron's balls. Aaron whimpered. Logan switched to the other leg, licking from knee to groin. Aaron wiggled, trying to get Logan's mouth where he wanted it. Logan ignored him and lapped at the juncture of each leg, paying particular attention to the nerve-rich skin that dipped inward on each side of his pelvis.

Aaron squirmed. "Damn it, Logan. Suck me."

Logan laughed, hot puffs of breath wafting over the wet tip of Aaron's dick. "Patience is a virtue, you know."

All that accomplished was making him yearn for the feel of Logan's hot, wet mouth all the more. "Fuck patience. Suck me. Do something, damn it."

Logan sat back in his chair and grabbed Aaron's hips, pulling him to the end of the table. He flung Aaron's calves over his shoulders and bent forward. Aaron held his breath, waiting to feel those firm pink lips wrap around the tip of his cock.

What he got was a long, wet lap between the cheeks of his ass. Aaron moaned and lifted his hips, silently begging for more. Logan's fingers sank into the soft flesh of his buttocks and spread them wide. He blew a stream of tepid air over the wetness left behind, causing tingles to race up Aaron's spine.

"Logan."

"I'm right here."

"Please."

"Please, what? Tell me what you want."

Aaron tried, but his response came out as a gurgled moan.

Logan flicked the tip of his tongue lightly over Aaron's fluttering hole. "This?" He laved over the tiny piece of flesh between Aaron's balls and ass. "This?" The flat of his tongue swiped up and over Aaron's balls. "Or maybe this? What do you want, baby? All you have to do is ask and it's yours. Tell me."

"Lick me."

Logan ran his tongue from asshole to scrotum. "Where?"

"My ass. Lick my ass."

Logan growled and swooped down, flicking his prehensile tongue over and around the quivering pucker of Aaron's asshole. He licked and laved, lapping at the tiny ring of muscle until Aaron felt his body relax, blossoming open like a flower, all his concentration on what Logan was doing to his ass. He felt warmth and wetness, a gentle lick and then a prod. He grunted, a strange garbled cry, as Logan began to put pressure on his hole. His hips rocked, pushing up, his cock riding air as Logan fucked him with his tongue. Nothing had ever felt so good.

Aaron's breath hitched in his chest. His balls contracted as if someone had zapped him with electricity, pulling tight to his groin, and he came. "I'm gonna… Oh, fuck yeah. Logan." With his head thrown back and his eyes squeezed closed, Aaron's body clenched down in orgasm. His cock spewed, firing his load in steamy ribbons across the rippling surface of his abdomen.

The flat of Logan's tongue gave one last swipe over Aaron's fluttering hole before moving up to gently lave his sac. Sensitive, the last of the aftershocks still ravaging his body, Aaron moaned and raised his head. Heavy-lidded eyes opened to peek down at Logan crouched between his splayed thighs.

Logan's tongue flicked over the base of Aaron's cock, making him shiver anew. "You're still hard."

"Uh-huh." Aaron watched his lover rise to his feet, his erection bobbing up and down. Logan's cock was flushed a deep shade of rose and weeping, the tip glistening with precome. Aaron licked his lips and sat up, sliding off the table

54

onto shaky legs. He pulled out the chair closest to him and crooked his finger at Logan. "Come here. Sit."

Eyes flaring with heat, Logan dropped down onto the chair without a word and Aaron straddled his lap. Their erections rubbed together as he leaned forward, desperate for a taste of his lover. Lips parted and clashed, tongues dueling as they kissed.

Logan's arms wrapped around Aaron's back, his palms kneading Aaron's ass cheeks and rocking their hips together. Without breaking their kiss, Aaron reached down between their torsos and slicked his hand up with the semen cooling on his stomach. He coated both their cocks in his come and grasped them with one hand, loosely stroking.

Logan moaned and pushed up with his hips, the base of his cock pressing into Aaron's balls, separating them, while the rest of his shaft caressed Aaron's dick. His arms vised around Aaron, holding him close and preventing him from moving his hand. "Stop."

Aaron whimpered and opened his eyes, breaking their kiss to stare down at Logan. "But…"

Logan leaned up to nip Aaron's bottom lip. "You're going to make me come if you keep that up. When I blow, I want it to be balls deep inside your tight little ass." His fingertips glided over Aaron's asshole, punctuating his words.

He wouldn't beg. He would not beg. "Do it. Fuck me."

Logan buried his face in the crook of Aaron's neck. "Shit. We need a condom. I don't have any. You don't happen to have one on you, do you?"

Aaron groaned. "No. I haven't been with anyone in… Hell, I can't even remember how long. I only wanted you."

One of Logan's hands rose to cup Aaron's face and pull him down for a tender kiss. "I only want you too. I haven't been with anyone since the divorce, and I couldn't tell you the last time I even had sex with Elaine before we separated. Things were bad for a long time before we finally split."

Aaron closed his eyes and kissed Logan again. He didn't want to think about Logan being with anyone else. "I'm clean. If you can trust me, we don't have to use one." A fresh rush of blood squeezed into his cock, making it that much harder, at the thought of Logan fucking him bare. He'd never done that before, with anyone, and it was a hell of a turn-on.

"Are you sure? I'm clean, too, I swear it, but you shouldn't—"

"I trust you. In all the time I've worked for you, I've never seen you intentionally hurt anyone. And I..." His face heated. "I really like the thought of feeling you come inside me."

Logan studied Aaron's face for a moment and then kissed him, ravaging his mouth with an intensity that stole his breath and the ability to think. He whimpered, his hips rocking. "Now, Logan. Fuck me now."

Logan patted him on the ass. "Stand up."

He stood, his legs embarrassingly wobbly. Logan skimmed the remaining come off Aaron's stomach and stroked it over his cock, making it glisten. He hunched down in the chair, sliding his ass to the very edge, and waggled his cock at Aaron. "You're in charge. Ride me."

Aaron lowered himself until he felt Logan's cock poking his balls. He leaned forward and felt it slide into the crack of his ass, the flared head glancing over his hole. Placing one hand on Logan's shoulder to brace himself, Aaron reached behind him and took hold of Logan's cock. He positioned the blunt head against the hungry entrance into his body and gently pressed down.

With Aaron's body still relaxed from being rimmed, Logan's widely flared cockhead popped through the tiny ring of muscle with little effort. Aaron gasped, the burning sting of seldom used muscles stretching to encompass Logan's swollen flesh bittersweet. Sweat beaded on his temples as he tried to relax his muscles and accept more of Logan's considerable length inside him.

Halfway down, Logan's hands bracketed Aaron's hips, stilling his downward momentum. His jaw was tense, his face flushed with the effort of holding back. "Hold still, baby. Just a second, please. You feel so damn good. Tight. Hot."

"Hurry, Logan. Want you so bad. Please." Aaron was beyond the point of caring about whether or not he sounded whiny. With half of Logan's dick inside him, it was all he could do to keep from rocking his hips.

Finally, Logan's grip loosened. Aaron put both hands on Logan's shoulders and shoved down, impaling himself to the hilt on Logan's thick cock. Aaron's head fell back, his entire consciousness centered on the feel of Logan buried inside him, his hard thighs underneath him, everywhere. "Oh, fuck. In me so goddamn deep, Logan. Feels so good."

He began to move, rising up until only the flared head was left inside him and then dropping back down, over and over. He dipped his head and kissed Logan, accepting his lover's tongue just as he accepted the stiff rigidity of his sex inside him. They shared breath, moving as one, as Logan held him close, one hand on Aaron's hip and the other rubbing tiny circles over every inch of skin it could reach. His back, the outside of his thigh, his abs and chest—nothing was spared from Logan's loving caress.

Logan's gentle touch, coupled with the fierce yet awed look on his face, pushed Aaron to move faster, to take them both higher. He pumped his hips harder. On every downward lunge, he squeezed his muscles around Logan's cock, relishing the knife-edge of pain that came with the pleasure.

The only sounds in the room were their labored breathing and the occasional grunt and moan each made. Logan's cries picked up speed and frequency. Aaron could feel the tension mounting in his lover's body and wanted to come with him when he finally spilled. He grasped his cock, pumping frantically. Logan's larger hand covered his own and together they stroked. Aaron angled his hips just right, letting Logan's cock peg his prostate, and that was it. A fountain of come sprayed out between their linked fingers. His anus contracted, squeezing down in time with each spurt, and tugged Logan over the precipice with him.

Logan's muscles locked up, his arms holding Aaron tight. He pushed up, burying as much of himself as he could deep inside Aaron and let go, anointing the slick walls of Aaron's channel with semen.

Aaron held on tight, never wanting to let go. As Logan's body trembled beneath his, Aaron slipped and said what he was thinking, the three little words no one should ever say during sex. "I love you."

Logan's body went rigid. Aaron bit his tongue, cursing himself for being foolish enough to blurt out what he was feeling. His hasty words ruined what was otherwise a beautiful moment. Things would be awkward between them now, and he hated that. Emotions made things sloppy, and he hated that, too. For a second, he thought of playing it off, pretending it was just something he said every time he got off, but he couldn't bring himself to say the words. He did love Logan, and though he wished he hadn't admitted to it, he wouldn't lie and say he didn't.

Aaron lifted up, freeing Logan's softening cock with a wet squelch. He tried to step back and avoid the uncomfortable scene that was sure to result from his declaration.

Logan's arms wrapped around him and wouldn't let go. "Where do you think you're going so fast?"

Aaron averted his eyes. "I have to…I need to go to the bathroom and get dressed. I have things to do today."

"You're right. You do have things to do today. You haven't fucked me yet."

Aaron's head whipped around. "What?"

Logan tugged Aaron back down onto his lap. "Well, it's only fair. I have to warn you, though, I've never bottomed before, so you might have to take things slow with me."

"Uh, Logan, I'm not really…I mean… It's just that I haven't ever…"

Logan pressed a quick kiss to his lips, hushing him. "You're adorable when you're flustered, you know that?" Logan hugged him tight. "Do you remember me saying I needed to tell you something before we got all carried away with other things?"

Damn, he'd forgotten all about that. "Yeah."

Logan met his nervous gaze and held it. "I'm in love with you, Aaron. I…I have been for a long time. Today wasn't just about sex, though that part was damn good too." Logan's

58

cheeks were tinged with pink. Aaron thought he'd never looked sweeter. "Shit. I'm screwing this up." He ran a hand over his hair, a habit Aaron recognized as something he did when he was flustered. "I want you. Not just in my bed, but in my life. The only reason I agreed to wait and tell you afterwards is because I didn't want you to think I was just saying whatever it took to get into your pants." The last sentence was blurted out so quick, the words tried to blend together.

Aaron's pulse thundered in his ears. A Cheshire grin spread across his face, and he attacked Logan, kissing him until they were both breathless and working on renewed erections. Aaron panted, "Say it again."

Logan kissed the tip of his nose and looked deep into his eyes. "I love you, Aaron, so, so much."

They hugged, and Aaron whispered the words he'd only moments before been so reluctant to admit. Only this time around, he had nothing to fear. Logan loved him back and Aaron knew without a shadow of a doubt that he'd never tire of telling Logan how much he meant to him. The start of a new, bright future loomed on the horizon, and Aaron couldn't wait for it to begin.

The End

CANDY MAN

Aaron opened the front door to a chorus of "trick or treat" from a small cluster of rag-tag children dressed in everything from a sheet to an elaborate princess costume.

"Oh, don't you guys look cute," he muttered for what had to be the thousandth time in the last several hours. When Logan had suggested staying in and handing out candy, instead of hitting the bars and dancing the night away, Aaron had given in with little fuss. He figured they would hand out chocolate until eight or nine and then be finished, leaving plenty of time for naughtier grown-up fun. Boy, was he wrong. At half-past eleven, the little rascals were still showing up on their doorstep.

Aaron shut the door, locked it, and turned off the porch light. He'd seen more than enough children tonight to last him until next year. If there were any other kids wandering around looking for candy, they were out of luck.

Tugging the snug rear end of his Batman costume out of his ass for the umpteenth time, he headed through the foyer and into the dark living room. He set the half-empty bowl of mini candy bars on the mantel and bent to turn on the gas fireplace. A flame roared to life, filling the dim room with dancing orange and black shadows. The perfect atmosphere for watching a scary movie on Halloween night.

Logan had disappeared upstairs earlier, after complaining for the umpteenth time about the uncomfortable cowboy outfit Aaron had talking him into wearing. Not that Aaron felt even slightly guilty about making his lover don skintight jeans, a pair of sexy-as-hell chaps, and a cowboy hat. The man was built like a brick shithouse and nothing showed off Logan's muscles more than tight jeans and a snug black T-shirt. The only thing better was Logan dressed in nothing but his skin. Unfortunately, having Logan wear his birthday suit while handing out Hershey bars didn't seem like the best idea, even if the thought had crossed his mind a time or ten while they'd been out shopping for costumes. If nothing else, it sure as hell would have livened up an otherwise boring evening.

Aaron's dick perked up and twitched inside the constrictive tights he had on under the Batman bodysuit and he briefly considered looking for his lover. The thought of catching Logan undressed, his beautifully rugged body on full display, and pouncing on the man held a lot of appeal, but Aaron quickly dismissed it. At the moment, all he wanted to do was slump down on the sofa and see what was on television.

But first, he needed to get rid of the spandex trying to squeeze his balls off. He tugged and pulled at the tight material, breathing out a deep sigh of relief as the bodysuit dropped to the floor and he stepped out of it. The tights were a bigger pain in the ass, pun intended, and wound up getting ripped down the middle in his hurry to take the damn things off.

I should have picked a more comfortable outfit.

The only reason he'd chosen the Batman theme was because he liked the way the tight fit made Logan's nostrils flare ever so slightly and his dark eyes spark with lust. Even after living in each other's back pockets for almost four months, the electrifying chemistry they shared still sometimes came as a shock to him. Logan was just so damn hot; it was hard for Aaron to believe someone so charismatic would fall in love with a geek like him. Not that Logan allowed Aaron a second to doubt their relationship. His lover was nothing if not consistent in the small things he did every day to remind Aaron that he cared. Aaron's own feelings had snowballed beyond the point of love, sometimes feeling so big he could hardly contain them. The need he felt for Logan hadn't dissipated one iota. If anything, it had only gotten stronger as they'd grown closer, learning all the ins and outs of private life with each other.

Aaron stepped over the heap of shiny black material—figuring he could clean up his mess later, when he got ready to go upstairs—and moved toward the couch. Cool air wafted over his bare skin, goose bumps popping up on his arms and legs as he made his way to the sofa. He flopped down on one end and dragged the comfy blue afghan off the back, spreading it out over the lower half of his body. With his back propped up against the arm of the couch and his legs stretched out across the length of the couch, Aaron picked up the remote and began flipping through the channels.

All the stations played horror movies on Halloween and he hated that he'd missed out on most of the good ones. When he came across the original Friday the 13th, he stopped and settled back to watch. Hopefully, Logan would come looking for him soon and they could snuggle and make out during the commercial breaks.

Aaron's eyelids grew heavy as he watched Jason chase a topless blonde on screen. His lips twisted into a wry smile, thinking about how silly it was for some woman to run around naked in the middle of the woods. Who came up with this crap anyway?

The floorboards overhead creaked, quickly followed by the sound of Logan jogging down the steps. "Aaron?"

"In here," Aaron called out, sitting up a little straighter, waiting for his lover to come into view.

Logan appeared in the doorway, his wide chest gloriously bare and a pair of light gray sweats hanging low on his lean hips. "Hey, babe. All finished with candy duty? Did you run out? Cause I think we still have another bag in the kitchen."

Aaron's gaze traveled down his lover's body to his bare feet before returning to the sizable bulge tenting out the front of the cotton pants. He licked his lips, his mouth suddenly filled with moisture. His cock jerked and began to fill, the nubby fabric of the afghan rubbing over the sensitive crown. Amazing how all it took was one look and he was ready to roll over and beg. "Yep. Done with the handing out, I mean. There's still some leftover chocolate in the bowl, if you want it. I just got tired of handing it out."

Logan strode across the room and leaned down for a kiss. Their mouths touched, soft and sweet, and Aaron whimpered. He slipped his tongue out and flicked it over the silky seam between Logan's lips. Logan's tongue met Aaron's with a quick warm and wet tap, and then his lover pulled away.

"So, where's the candy? I have a bit of a sweet tooth to-night."

"Mmm," Aaron replied, trying to remember where he'd put the bowl, as he ran the back of his fingers over the hard outline of Logan's dick. "You have to say trick or treat first."

Logan grinned. "Trick or treat. Give me something good to eat…" His singsong voice broke off as he cracked up, chuckling at the childish song.

"God, you're a goofball."

"Yeah, well, I'm your goofball."

Aaron held back the smile trying to spread across his face and faked a long, drawn out sigh. "I suppose you are. Though Lord knows why I put up with you."

Logan seemed to think on that for a minute, then he grinned, the expression more wicked than humorous. "Well, it could be because you love me." He pulled down the front of his sweats, allowing the thick length of his fat, uncut cock to jut skyward. "Or maybe you only put up with me for this."

Aaron's gaze zeroed in on Logan's groin and watched as his lover stroked up and down the thick shaft. Foreskin moved back and forth, revealing the damp tip of Logan's crown on every pass. Moisture caught the roving light from the fire, making the crown glisten, and Aaron's mouth began to water. He reached out for Logan, who stepped back just out of his reach.

"Ah ah ah. You didn't say the magic word."

"Please." Aaron suppressed a growl of frustration and reached for his lover again. Instead of moving to stand beside the couch, as Aaron had expected, Logan straddled his hips.

He leaned forward and brushed a curl from Aaron's forehead. "What do you want, baby? Want me to fuck you, hard and fast, over the arm of the couch? Suck you off, let you suck me?"

"How about all of the above?"

"Feeling greedy tonight, are we?"

Aaron rubbed his palms over the firm musculature of Logan's chest, feeling every bump and ridge, each indentation of his washboard stomach. "For you? Always." He moved his hand further down and skated his forefinger over the damp tip of Logan's cock, pulling away moisture. He popped the digit in his mouth and sucked it clean, groaning as the flavor of his lover's need exploded over his tongue.

"Fuck, that's sexy." Logan ran his fingers gently over Aaron's lips, starting at the bow if his upper lip and ending with the full curve of the lower. "How do you want me, baby? I need you."

Aaron met Logan's eyes. "I want to suck you. Want you to fuck my mouth and come for me."

A curse passed Logan's lips as he bent, taking Aaron's mouth in a fast, hard kiss. Their lips worked together in tandem, moving and rubbing, their tongues dueling in passion. By the time Logan pulled away, Aaron was panting. His hips shifted restlessly, searching for friction.

"Damn, I love kissing you. You taste so good. I could do it all night, if you didn't make me so horny." Logan pressed another quick kiss to Aaron's lips.

Aaron groaned as Logan shifted, his legs rubbing against Aaron's cock as he squirmed out of his sweats, one leg at a time, and dropped them to the floor. When he was finished, with every gloriously naked inch of him on display, Logan scooted up Aaron's body. Aaron worked with him, wiggling down in an effort to get closer to the object of his desire. Aaron ended up with Logan's knees on either side of his chest and a heavy cock directly in line with his mouth.

He shot a brief glance up at Logan and noted the intense expression on his lover's face, before his focus returned to the stiff cock in his face. Wet tipped and dripping with need, Logan's cock called for all of Aaron's attention. Saliva filled his mouth as he lifted his neck and ran his lips down one side of Logan's prick and back up the other, wetting the wide shaft.

"Oh yeah, that's it. Lick my cock. Get it good and wet, baby." Logan moaned and rocked his hips, begging for more. Aaron obliged and lapped at the silken skin, salivating over every hard inch. When he reached the base, Aaron strained forward to tease the root of Logan's cock with the tip of his tongue.

Logan pulled back and fisted his cock, pressing the blunt end against Aaron's mouth. "Enough teasing. Suck me off." Logan's voice was gruff; his words more of a demand than a request. Not that Aaron was about to argue. There was nothing he liked more than to take Logan in his mouth, to be the only one who could wring such pleasure from his lover's body.

Aaron pushed his tongue against the tiny, winking slit and lapped away all the moisture he could find before running it over and around the broad cap. He delved beneath Logan's foreskin with the tip of his tongue and lapped at the flared rim with tiny flicks, pulling a desperate groan from his lover's mouth. That sound coupled with the tiny hip thrusts Logan was making only served to egg Aaron on. He sucked harder, working Logan's cockhead with his tongue, keeping the pressure tight around the shaft.

Logan pushed in and out with short, shallow thrusts that rubbed the sensitive underside of his dickhead over the flat of Aaron's tongue, depositing silky, bittersweet drops of moisture with every pass.

All too soon, Logan's body stiffened and he groaned, the ragged sound loud in the otherwise quiet room. "Jesus, Aaron, don't stop. I'm gonna…"

Aaron dropped his head back, keeping only the uppermost inches of Logan in his mouth, and began to twist his mouth from side to side, working the tip in tight circles. Logan's cock swelled larger against Aaron's tongue, every beat of his lover's heart perceivable through the fragile, silken skin. Aaron laved the tip, teasing the bundle of nerves just under the head, and felt Logan's body shudder. The first forceful gush of cum took him by surprise, although he'd expected it, and made Aaron choke. He forced his gag reflex into submission and suckled at Logan's knob, swallowing the remaining cum down without any problem. He kept at it until Logan began to soften, wanting all of Logan's passion, every single drop he could coax out of the man he loved.

Finally, Logan sighed and shuffled backward, pulling his cock from between Aaron's lips with squishy pop. He bent and kissed Aaron, licking the remaining cum from his lips as he settled into a comfortable position. "Damn, you're good at that. You're going to kill me with that mouth one of these days."

Aaron grinned and nipped at Logan's bottom lip. "You know you love it."

Logan cupped Aaron's cheek. "I do. Not as much as I love you, though."

Aaron's breath hitched at the love shining so clearly in his lover's eyes. He caught Logan's hand where it lay against his cheek and pressed a kiss into the center of the palm. "I love you too, Logan."

"Good. Now where's the candy you promised me, you tease?"

"Tease?" Aaron shook his head, amused. "Why am I the tease, when you've already gotten off once, and I'm still laying here suffering from an aching dick? How does that work?"

"You're the one who promised to share chocolate, if I let you suck me off." He reached down and cupped Aaron's cock and balls through the afghan separating their lower torsos. "I'll be happy to help you out with that in any way you want, just as soon as you give up the candy bars."

Aaron groaned. "You're an evil, evil man."

"Maybe so, but you love me."

"Fine. Have it your way. The leftover candy is on the mantel. Help yourself."

Logan hopped up and strode across the room, giving Aaron a spectacular view of his muscular back and tight ass as it flexed with every step. He grabbed the bowl off the mantel, snatched out one of the little candy bars out and tore it open. "Uh, babe?"

Aaron rolled onto his side and propped his head up with his hand, elbow against the couch beneath him. "Hmm?"

"You might want to think twice about laying stuff up here from now. These are all melted."

"Sorry." Aaron shrugged one shoulder. "I didn't think about it. I'm sure it still tastes the same; just lick it out of the wrapper."

Logan stuck the whole candy bar, wrapper and all, inside his mouth and slowly pulled it back out, devoid of chocolate. "Still good."

Aaron moaned. Jesus, that's sexy. A wanton streak flooded over him and he laid a hand over his own dick through the afghan. "I've got something good for you right here."

"Oh you do, do you?" Logan raised a single winged, black brow. "Something as delicious as chocolate?"

"Even better." Aaron blushed even as he pulled back the cover and fisted the pale shaft of his cock. He felt Logan's gaze on him, a phantom caress, as he lifted one knee and bared himself completely, giving his prick one long stroke from root to crown. He ran his thumb through the pearly drop gathered at the tip and brought it to his mouth, sucking it clean. Aaron's eyelids drooped as the salty taste of sex burst over his taste buds.

"Mmm…" He moaned theatrically, his hand going back to is dick and working it over, really playing it up for Logan's benefit. "You don't know what you're missing out on."

Logan growled. The pulsating noise caused Aaron's ass to clench. He knew just what that sexy sound felt like against his lips, around his dick. It never failed to turn him on, to make him need—badly—and now was no exception. His hips shifted restlessly under Logan's intense scrutiny. "God, Logan. Come over here and touch me. Please."

Logan prowled across the room toward Aaron. He dropped the bowl next to the couch and went to his knees. "Quit." He swatted Aaron's hand away from his erection and fingered the wet tip. "This is mine."

"Prove it."

"Gladly." Logan swooped in and swallowed Aaron down, taking him all the way in until Aaron could feel the smooth, wet muscles at the back of Logan's throat undulating against the sensitive tip of his cock.

"Holy fuck, Logan." Aaron slammed his head back, his eyes falling closed as pleasure crashed through his body. His hips rocked up of their own volition as he tried to bury his cock deeper in the sweltering pleasure of his lover's hot mouth. "Oh, God. So good, baby."

"Mmm…" Logan groaned around Aaron's prick, the vibration doing wonderful things around his shaft as Logan bobbed his head up and down. Logan's hand joined his mouth on Aaron's cock and both began to work in sync, squeezing and sucking and…

Aaron's ballsac drew tight, his nuts hugging his body. "Oh. So close. Don't stop."

Logan pulled off with a wet squelch and licked his lips. He glanced up at Aaron, his lips swollen from sucking. "You taste good." He ran the back of his fingers over Aaron's balls and patted him on the leg. "Hang on a sec, okay?"

Logan's attention dropped to the floor and a rustling noise filled the air. Aaron lifted his head and looked over the edge of the couch to see Logan peeling open a candy bar.

Aaron rolled his eyes and dropped his head back against the arm of the sofa. "Logan, do you really think now is the time to feed your sweet tooth? I'm dying over here."

Logan didn't even look up. "Be patient, baby."

"Whatever," Aaron muttered in aggravation. He grabbed his cock and started stroking, working the tip good and hard the way he liked it. If Logan wasn't going to help him out he'd just take care of it himself. He wasn't willing to wait another second.

Just as he got into a good rhythm, his hand sliding just right over his shaft, Logan grabbed his forearm, halting any further movement. "Aren't you forgetting something?"

Damn it, I was so close. Aaron blew out a deep breath. "No." He tried to jerk his arm away from Logan with little result. "Let me go, asshole. One of us has to finish what you started."

"Jesus, you're a bossy little thing." Logan grasped Aaron's free wrist and guided them both up over his head. "Hold them there."

"Why?"

"Just do it."

"You better not be playing with me, Logan. I need to come." Aaron glared at Logan but did as he was asked.

Logan laid his arm across Aaron's stomach, an opened gooey Hershey's bar in his hand, and kissed Aaron's abs, right beneath his belly button. "I'm not going to leave you hanging, baby. I promise."

Aaron tensed, waiting to see what Logan was up to. He hadn't been joking about the need to come. His balls ached and his dick felt like a lead pipe where it lay against his abdomen, steadily leaking precum.

Logan leaned up and kissed him. Aaron's eyelids lowered as their lips connected, only to fly back open as he felt something warm and wet rub over his chest. He glanced down and saw a long smear of brown underneath his left nipple. "Damn it. Watch what you're doing, Logan. You're going to get chocolate all over me."

Logan grinned, his pearly white teeth a startling contrast against the flushed pink of his lips. "That's the idea."

Aaron stiffened, and though he didn't think it was possible for his cock to get any harder, he could've sworn he felt more blood trying to pump into his shaft, stretching the already uncomfortably tight skin. He held still, barely breathing, and watched as Logan covered both his nipples with chocolate and then painted a thin trail of it down the middle of his abs, stopping just short of the trimmed curls wreathing his dick.

Logan licked the chocolate from Aaron's skin, his warm tongue sliding through the sweet confection with little flicks interspersed with long, slow laps.

"Jesus, Logan." Aaron gulped and squirmed a little, the muscles in his stomach rippling.

"Mm hmm. Like that, don't you, baby?"

"God, yes. More."

Logan licked him from nipple to belly button, his lips and tongue lapping at every inch of skin between. Aaron wiggled and panted, his arms flung above his head, feeling slutty and decadent as his lover teased and played with his body.

Aaron lifted his head. "What, no chocolate for my dick?" He teased.

Logan glanced up, his mouth hovering over Aaron's erection. "Don't need any. This tastes good enough all by itself."

Logan's head slowly descended. Humid air wafted over the swollen crown of Aaron's cock a second before Logan's lips finally surrounded the tip. The hot, silky wetness of Logan's tongue bathed the blunt cap and poked at the slit, prodding every nerve ending in Aaron's dick to life.

Aaron whimpered, mesmerized by the sight of Logan's dark head at his groin, his lover's full lips wrapped around his shaft, swallowing him one slow inch at a time. It was a toss up for which excited him more: the hot press of tongue and lips around his shaft, or the sight of Logan's lips spread wide around his dick, his lover's mouth moving up and down and leaving his shaft glistening with saliva.

If it weren't for the underlying thrum of need coursing through his veins, he could've stayed in that position forever, content just to feel Logan's hands on him, touching him and loving him. As it stood, he didn't think that was going to be possible much longer. His need rode him strong, the same way he longed for Logan to do. He needed to feel Logan inside him, to come with his lover.

The mouth around his cock gave one last, long suck and popped off. Logan's mouth moved lower and nuzzled Aaron's balls, licking and tugging the wrinkled sac. Saliva dripped down his balls and meandered through his crease, wetting him

71

down. Logan's fingers followed the moisture, gliding over the crack of his ass. The blunt edge of one digit ringed Aaron's hole and applied the slightest teasing pressure. The tip slipped inside and wiggled, massaging around and around the tense ring of muscle in slow, circular motions.

Aaron's body throbbed with impatience. He pushed down, trying to force Logan's finger deeper inside him. "God, yes. More. Give me more."

"Anything you want, love."

One finger became two and then three, stretching Aaron open with gentle persuasion. He rocked against them, forcing his ass down harder on Logan's thick digits. His hole burned and clenched with an all encompassing need for more.

"So tight, baby. I can't wait to feel you pulsing around my cock, milking me with your ass."

The tone of Logan's voice—deep and hoarse, laden with desire—inflamed Aaron even more than the naughty words did. He bucked against the fingers in his ass, wanting more. Aaron grasped his legs behind each knee and pulled them back against his chest, opening himself to Logan. "Please, Logan. I want you. Fuck me. Now."

"I'm all yours, baby. I love you."

Logan's fingers slid away, making Aaron cry out at their loss. He was shushed with a quick kiss and then Logan was moving backward, kneeling between Aaron's thighs. The broad tip of Logan's cock touched Aaron's entrance. He pushed down and felt his hole stretch, making room for his lover to enter his body. Letting out a deep breath, Aaron felt his muscles ease and allow Logan's thick crown to slide inside him. He moaned, unable to hold the sound back, and shuddered as Logan steadily pushed deeper.

Logan leaned forward, pressing Aaron's legs against his chest, and swept his tongue over Aaron's bottom lip. His hands wandered up and down Aaron's chest, pinching his nipples and petting his belly. "Fuck. So good. You feel so good, baby."

"Uh huh," Aaron muttered, overwhelmed by the feel of Logan all around him, on top of him and inside, filling him to

72

bursting. They kissed, lost in a vortex of heat and pleasure, soft moans peppering the air.

With every slow drag out and thrust back in, Aaron's desire soared higher. Logan fucked him with long and slow lunges that nudged his prostate with every pass. In and out, on and on, Logan invaded him until Aaron's world narrowed to just the two of them, his lover's body feeling more like an extension of his own than a separate entity.

He let go of his legs and wrapped them around Logan's hips in favor of touching. His hands slid over Logan's damp back and settled on his ass, gripping the firm, flexing mounds while Logan slammed into him.

Aaron's entire body tensed, all his muscles straining toward the same goal. Above him, Logan's strong form glistened with sweat, his muscles rippling with every deep lunge forward. Logan's penetrating gaze never left Aaron's face, his lover's eyes saying all the words his mouth didn't as they labored toward joined ecstasy.

Logan's groin spanked Aaron's ass, his thrusts coming harder and faster. The cock inside Aaron swelled and bucked, Logan's seed filling him up at the same time Logan cried out, his voice hoarse. He lunged hard and buried himself to the balls inside Aaron.

Aaron keened, his back arching as every muscle in his body clenched tight. The world went white around the edges, his brain filling with electric snow as his body clenched and released, the force of his orgasm taking his breath away. He panted and rode the waves, trying to hold on to Logan tight with fingers that slid over his lover's sweaty back.

Logan rolled off him, making Aaron wiggle to the edge of the couch in order to make room for them both on the narrow cushions. Warm arms wrapped around him before he could move far and tugged him against Logan's broad chest. Aaron pressed his face against Logan's breastbone and listened to the steady thump of Logan's strong heart, amazed as always that he'd fallen in love with a man so fine, and had that love returned ten-fold.

Logan's hand carded through Aaron's damp hair. "Jesus. Making love to you just keeps getting better and better. I think you actually melted my bones this time."

Aaron smiled against Logan's skin. "Well, better you than the rest of the chocolate."

The End

EYE CANDY

Chapter One

Jake Remora stormed into the antique store, Time and
Again, with a scowl on his face. Bells chimed noisily overhead
as he entered; the door slapped shut behind him with a loud
thump.

The proprietor, Sam Goode, was a contrary asshole two
clicks shy of being older than God and twice as ornery. Sam
had left a message on Jake's cell phone, claiming there were
delays in the arrival of the antique French Burl armoire he'd
ordered for one of his clients. Since Jake was counting on that
piece to finish up a project, he was not a happy camper. He
didn't appreciate having to make excuses for why he was late
finishing a job. Interior Design by Jake was his baby; he
couldn't allow someone to fuck with its reputation. Heads
were going to roll if there wasn't a damn good reason for the
holdup.

He stomped toward the front counter, his gaze combing the small interior of the shop. Although he vaguely recalled an open sign on the front door, and the inside lights were on, not a single sign of life stirred within the building. Quiet as a grave, the air was redolent of old books and wood, lending to the tomblike atmosphere.

Undeterred, Jake reached the waist-high counter and leaned across it. "Hey, Sam! Quit hiding in the back, and get your crusty old ass out here. I need the piece I ordered."

A door slammed, followed immediately by silence. Impatience thrummed through him as he stood upright and tapped the rounded toe of his new, chocolate-colored leather Gucci biker boots on the chipped linoleum floor. "Come on, man. I don't have all day." A blemish on the cuff of his white cashmere sweater caught his attention. He picked at the navy-colored stain, disgusted to see what looked like ink on his clothing.

Christ. Can't people clean up after them-fucking-selves? The sound of footsteps reached Jake's ears. He looked up, expecting to see Sam coming through the door in his trademark overalls and red flannel shirt. Instead, a young blond wearing a black T-shirt and ragged jeans pushed through the swinging door. Judging by the lack of lines around the man's wide blue eyes and a hint of light brown stubble on the lower half of his round face, Jake guessed him to be in his early twenties.

"I'm sorry you had to wait. It seems like no one ever comes in until I have to take a leak." The blond grinned, and sweet, little dimples appeared on either side of his plump, pink lips. "What can I do for you?"

Drop to your knees and open wide, was on the tip of Jake's tongue. "I wasn't waiting long." He thrust his hand across the counter. "I'm Jake. And you are?"

The young man maintained eye contact as he took Jake's hand in his own and gave it a firm shake. The rough pads of his fingers lingered as he slowly pulled away. "I'm Jimmy, Sam's grandson. Pops had to leave early today   he had a doctor appointment   but I can help you with whatever you need."

I'm sure you can. "I need to check on the status of an order I placed a while back for an armoire." Suddenly, throwing a bitch-fit didn't seem quite so urgent. After all, it wasn't as if a few choice words would make the piece of furniture appear any faster.

"Um, okay. I'm afraid Pops doesn't believe in updating the store for the twenty-first century, so he doesn't have a computer that lists his inventory. If you can describe it though, I could go into the back and take a look around for you. See if it's in."

"Or, better yet," Jake interrupted, "I could just come back with you. We could both look for it." And see what comes up in the interim. "That would be easier than describing the armoire. Quicker, too."

Jimmy cast a glance back at the storeroom and then at Jake. He blushed. "I'm not so sure about that. Pops doesn't like for anyone to mess around with his things."

"I wouldn't have to touch anything, unless you want me to." Jake met Jimmy's gaze, held it, and licked his lips suggestively, testing the waters. He could be way off base, but the curious gleam in Jimmy's eyes spoke of more than casual interest. The blushing was cute, and a dead giveaway that the other man was interested. "No one has to find out about anything that happens while Sam's out." The old man would shit a cookie if he found out his grandson was batting for Jake's team. Homophobic jackass.

Jimmy blinked. A flush crept up his neck and steadily spread across his cheeks. "I...um..."

"I'm really good at keeping secrets, Jimmy."

Straight white teeth bit into the plump center of Jimmy's lower lip. He nodded. "Follow me." He turned and walked through the door. Jake followed, his dick swelling to attention as his gaze locked on the prize snuggled beneath faded denim.

Jimmy had a fabulous ass: high and tight, like two firm peaches. The analogy made him wonder if Jimmy's cheeks would be covered in fuzz or bare. He always preferred to fuck a smooth ass, but he wasn't choosy. As long as it was attached to a healthy, attractive man, he was game. Living in a town full of horny college students certainly had its perks, and he wasn't above indulging himself in whatever he could get his hands on.

Jake waited until the door swung shut behind them before he pounced. He crowded Jimmy against the wall, cupped his jaw in one hand, and moved in for a kiss. He'd no more than pressed their lips together when Jimmy pushed against his chest.

"Stop. Nothing personal, but I don't kiss."

"Okay. Whatever." Jake felt a little puckish as he spun Jimmy around to face the wall. If the kid didn't want to kiss, who was he to force it on him? They'd just skip the pleasantries and get right down to it.

He buried his face in the curve of Jimmy's throat and licked a long path from the base of his neck up to the meaty lobe of his ear. Mmm…salty. Jimmy smelled of soap, wood, and light hint of sweat   musky and damn near perfect. If there was a better scent in the world, Jake would have been hard-pressed to think of one.

"Don't leave a mark," Jimmy whispered, grinding his ass back against the front of Jake's slacks.

"I won't." Jake reached around Jimmy, intent on ridding the younger man of his excess clothing, and found Jimmy's fly already open. He peeked over the other man's shoulder and saw a well-proportioned cock, cut and a little on the thin side, jutting above the waistband of plain tighty whiteys. Jimmy grasped the base of his narrow shaft and worked it up and down.

Jimmy shot a sultry look over his shoulder. "Like it?"

"You'll do." Jake gave him a wink, grabbed the sides of Jimmy's pants, and tugged them and his underwear down in one fell swoop. The pert ass he revealed—the cheeks so firm and tight they clung together and hid the valley between—was almost enough to bring him to his knees.

"Nice," he commented, his hands already at the clasp of his slacks. Locked inside its cloth cage, Jake's prick was more than ready to be set free.

Jake hastily pulled a condom and pillow pack of lube from his right front pocket, while his other hand worked the release on his pants. He unzipped and tugged his dick and balls out, letting the heavy weight of his sac rest atop the elastic band of his boxer briefs. He shoved his bare dick in the furrow between Jimmy's taut cheeks, relishing the immense heat pouring from the other man's skin as he rubbed against him. "Want me?" God knew he was about to burst he was so ready to bury himself inside the other man. Jimmy was hot for it, and just his type—easy.

"God, yes." Jimmy pressed his ass back into Jake's crotch and ground against him. "Do it. Fuck me."

Go me, Jake thought, as he backed, allowing himself enough room to work with the condom. I've barely touched him, and he's already reduced to two-word sentences.

With steady hands, he rolled the condom down over his shaft and secured it at the base. He tore the lube packet open and squeezed out half its contents into his palm, smearing the slick goo over his dick. He enjoyed the feel of his hand around his stiff prick for half a second before the lure of burying himself balls deep inside the tempting ass in front of him regained prominence.

"Spread your ass for me," Jake demanded, wringing the last of the lube into his cupped hand.

Jimmy's forehead and shoulder thumped the wall as he pulled his cheeks apart, four thick fingers framing the tender pink skin of his crease. "Like this?"

"Perfect." Jake groaned, his gaze locked on the rosette of Jimmy's anus and the sparse whirl of light brown hair surrounding the crinkled pucker. "Fuck. I love your ass," he murmured then worked the remaining lube over and into the tight little hole with one finger. Too impatient to use much finesse, he quickly added another. Slick heat gripped his fingers and squeezed, giving his dick a preview of how damn tight it would be once he got inside the other man's passage. He gave his fingers a twist, searching…

"Shit." Jimmy moaned and jerked, riding Jake's fingers. "Quit teasing, man. Fuck me."

"Never let it be said that I left a man wanting." Jake pulled his fingers out with a wet squelch and lined up his prick. His pulse skipped a beat, taking in the way the broad head of his cock loomed over Jimmy's tiny hole, ready to split it open. He pushed all the way in with one steady shove, watching as his cock disappeared, inch by slow, pleasurable inch.

God, that was hot.

He grunted as sweet pressure sucked at his shaft like a hungry mouth, and pressed up against the other man's broad back. "Damn, you're tight." Kissing the sensitive dip under Jimmy's ear, he asked, "Feel good?"

"Yeah. Move. Give it to me."

"You got it." Jake got a good grip on Jimmy's narrow waist and held on as he inched his hips backward until the flared rim of his cock stopped him. Jimmy's asshole also re-sisted his effort to disengage their bodies. He lunged back inside, hard and fast, and then did it again, setting a violent pace that made his dick ache and his balls bounce. Jimmy worked with him, pushing back into every thrust and whimper-ing for more. Jake's dick felt like it was being crushed inside the tight inferno. Fuck, it felt good. He rolled his hips and pro-pelled his dick in and out, over and again, and chased the orgasm hovering just out of reach.

"Christ." Jimmy bucked, the walls of his ass undulating around Jake's shaft. One of Jimmy's hands slammed into the wall and fisted against the drywall, bracing his weight, as the other sped up along his cock and jerked it in short, rough yanks. "Right there, man. Harder."

Making a mental note of where "right there" was, Jake made it his personal goal to pound the shit out of that spot. He kept at it, working Jimmy's ass for all the sensation he could get. Perspiration beaded on his face and neck, his sweater growing damp. He powered in and out, his lungs bellowing as he moved faster, putting everything he had into each thrust.

His balls began to burn and lift, pressure building inside him. "God," Jake whispered. "I'm close. Gonna come." Leav-ing one hand on Jimmy's hip for leverage, Jake reached around Jimmy with the other and latched onto his slender, upthrust cock with a firm grip. They tugged together in long, full strokes.

Jake panted, so close to coming, but determined to hold off until he felt the other man climax first. Just when he didn't think he was going to make it—his balls felt like they were trying to crawl inside his groin, and his dick swollen passed the point of no return—Jimmy's ass clenched around his cock. Contractions squeezed his shaft in time with the slick pulses of fluid spurting over his hand.

Thank fuck. Jake closed his eyes, his mind drained of everything but the need to come, and shoved home. He bucked, jerking as the first wave of release rushed over him, and let his load fly inside the snug grip of the condom.

Jake was the first to recover. He eased out of Jimmy's ass—the other man's whimper almost enough to tempt him into asking for a second go-round—and pulled himself together. "You okay?"

Jimmy didn't budge from where he leaned against the wall, panting. "Yeah. I'm good. Thanks."

Okay. Jake divested himself of the used condom, wrinkling his nose at the mess, and tied it off. He left his wet dick hanging out of his slacks. "Uh, is there a bathroom back here I can use?"

"Sure." Jimmy waved toward the left. "Just, um, flush it, okay? I don't want anyone to see it."

Jake was a little unnerved by the way the guy refused to look at him, but it wasn't the first time he'd slept with someone who didn't want to talk afterward. It probably wouldn't be the last. Hit-it-and-quit-it sex was prevalent for a reason, even if this encounter wasn't quite of the anonymous variety.

He toddled into the bathroom and cleaned up. When he came out, Jimmy was nowhere to be seen. Jake thought about looking for him, just to see if he was okay, but figured what the hell. Jimmy was a big boy, and Jake hadn't been all that rough with him. If the dude had wanted to face him, he wouldn't have disappeared.

Jake walked out of the shop into the brisk, spring sunshine and headed for his truck. He may not have gotten the armoire he went in for, but the recompense had been damn fine.

Chapter Two

His cell phone rang as Jake shifted the truck gear into reverse. With his foot on the brake, he picked it up and glanced at the caller ID. The number for Time and Again blazed across the display screen. Hitting the ignore option, he sent the call to voice mail and turned his attention to the task at hand.

It wasn't the first time Jimmy had called him in the week since they'd fucked, and it probably wouldn't be the last, but he had more important things to do than explain the virtues of sport fucking to Jimmy. He hoped the kid would take the hint and leave him alone. He was becoming a nuisance.

Watching for Logan's directions through the side mirror, Jake began to back his truck up to the porch. When Logan held his hand up to stop, Jake threw the truck into park and killed the engine. He hopped out of the cab and headed toward Logan, who leaned against the wooden handrail that led up to the redwood deck.

The couch Aaron had asked him to order was in the truck bed, strapped down with bungee cords to keep it from sliding around on the way over to the new house Aaron and Logan had bought together. Jake was helping Aaron out with the decorating, getting him discounts here and there whenever he could swing it.

"Damn, I'm glad that ride's over. Why on earth did you two have to pick a house even farther out in the boonies than the old one?"

Logan shrugged. "We like our privacy."

Jake leaned against the other side of the stairs. "Make Aaron scream loud and often, do you?"

"Wouldn't you like to know?"

"Know what?" Aaron came bouncing out of the house and rushed Logan, throwing his arms around his lover's waist.

"Nothing." Logan turned Aaron around, draped his arms over Aaron's shoulders, pulled him back against him, and rested his head on the wild puff of red curls atop the shorter

82

man's head. "Jake here was just inquiring about our sex life, is all."

"Oh, really?" Aaron turned his gaze on Jake, his bright green eyes twinkling mischievously. "Why so curious, Jake? You want to join in or something?"

"Sure, I wouldn't mind helping out a time or two, if your old man can't do the job anymore."

"Over my dead body, asshole." Logan smiled, tightening his arms around Aaron.

Aaron, the little rascal, winked at Jake before dropping his head back to gaze up at Logan. "You know, being the filling in a twin brother sandwich does sound pretty hot."

Logan's chocolate eyes, so much like Jake's own, flashed with dark heat. He lowered his head and kissed Aaron hard, as if the kid's tongue was made of filet mignon and Logan was suffering from iron deficiency.

Jake squirmed, uncomfortable with the hard-on rapidly developing behind his fly. He felt slightly ill at his physical reaction to watching his brother make out, until he rationalized that it was only Aaron making him hard. Well, that and watching Aaron suck face with someone who was the mirror image of himself.

He and Logan had the same swarthy complexion, dark eyes, and big, honking nose. People seldom noticed that Logan's shoulders were a little broader and Jake's frame a little leaner from all the hours he spent running and at the gym. Take away Logan's constant wardrobe of jeans and T-shirts, give him a few extra inches of hair so his naturally wavy locks would reach his shoulders like Jake's did, and people wouldn't be able to tell them apart. Unless Logan opened his mouth, that is. His brother definitely had the domineering older sibling thing down pat, whereas Jake tried to remain low key and laid back.

Aaron, on the other hand, was adorable with his curly red hair, freckles, and perpetually sweet demeanor. Jake had always thought so. Logan was lucky Jake hadn't scooped the kid right out from underneath his nose during the four years Aaron had pined away for his brother. The only thing that had held

Jake back was that Aaron would have expected more from him than a damn good orgasm or three.

No, he thought, watching as they broke apart, Logan deserves all the bliss he's found. Lord knew the man had suffered, living half his life in the closet, to get where he was today. Jake wouldn't begrudge his brother a moment of that happiness.

"Nice to see you're finally coming up for air," Jake teased, as they finally broke apart. "I was starting to think I'd have to get out the hose in order to break the two of you apart."

Aaron's face flamed, but Logan just snorted. "What the matter, baby brother? Jealous?"

"Baby brother by all of seven whole minutes, jerk off. And fuck no, I'm not jealous." Much. He couldn't help but wonder what it was like on the other side of things   having someone to come to home to every night who wanted you for more than just your dick. He gave a mental snort. Nah, that's not for me. "You two are just sickening, with all that lovey-dovey crap. Shouldn't the honeymoon phase be over by now? Frankly, I'm surprised Aaron hasn't killed you. I remember what a pain your ugly ass was to live with when we were growing up."

"Hey!" Aaron lifted his head, his pointed chin rising. "That's my ass now, and I'll have you know it's anything but ugly."

"Thanks, babe." Logan beamed a mega-kilowatt smile down at Aaron and bent to kiss him again.

Jake made gagging noises, poking a little good-natured fun at them, and went to unstrap the couch. They were still going at it when he finished, so he cleared his throat loudly. "How about a hand here, guys? Think you can cool it down long enough to help me get this bitch of a couch inside the house?"

Aaron pulled away from Logan. "What can I do to help?"

Jake climbed up into the back of the truck and pitched down two clear, oversized bags containing the sofa cushions. "Here. You can take these. Logan and I can get the couch."

Aaron caught the bags with an oomph. "Got 'em. Thanks again for ordering this monster for me. The couch is the last piece of furniture we needed to complete the living room."

Logan sidled up to the tailgate. "Thank God it'll be done. I was getting sick of having to sit all the way across the room from you. The suede recliners you picked out are great, but I still don't see why you insisted on keeping them separated when there was no sofa to put in between them before now."

"Because," Aaron said with an eye roll, "I wanted to keep everything where it was suppose to be, whether we had all the furniture or not. You don't hear me complaining about that extra leaf you want to keep in the middle of the dining room table, even though we hardly need room for ten people every night, do you?"

"But you just did, didn't you?" Logan swatted Aaron on the ass before reaching for his end of the sofa. "Would you mind holding the door open for us, babe?"

"Yeah, sure. Just let me"—he held up the bags—"get rid of these."

Aaron turned as he started up the steps. "Remember to lift with your legs."

"Yes, dear," Logan parroted with a wry grin.

Jake observed the way Logan mooned over Aaron, his brother's gaze locked on the other man until he disappeared into the house. "You know you're both so mushy you're disgusting, right?"

Logan turned his attention to Jake and the sofa. "Oh, yeah." A goofy smile spread across Logan's face. "You should try it sometime. There's more to life than casual sex, you know?"

"I went that route once, and you know what happened. Never again. I'm happy for you, but monogamous bliss isn't for me."

One of Logan's eyebrows quirked. "That didn't used to be the case. You forget, I'm one of the few people who can remember what you were like before you turned into the jaded slut you are today. Back when you used to walk around with your head in the clouds and pine over "

"Shut up, Logan. The past is in the past, where it belongs."

"Whatever, Jake. I was just saying..." Logan shrugged. "Seems to me that someone who's put the past behind them and moved on wouldn't get so damn defensive every time it's brought up."

"Could we just can the chitchat and get on with moving this damn couch? I didn't come out there to have my love life psychoanalyzed by the likes of you, Dr. Phil." Jake got behind the couch and shoved it forward, forcing Logan to jump back and catch it before it tilted over and hit the ground.

"Fine, asshole. Excuse me for giving a shit." Logan hefted the sofa higher, trying to get a better grip on it. "And for your information, you don't have a love life. All you have is a sex life. There is a difference, you know."

"Fuck you, Logan." Jake gave the sofa another push, taking out some of his frustration on it before he said something he'd regret later. Just because Logan wanted to take a stroll down memory lane didn't mean he had to go along for the ride. Some things were better left forgotten. He didn't think Logan would appreciate it if he brought up his ex-wife every time he was trying to make a point.

"Quit shoving the fuckin' sofa. If you make me drop this end, I'm going to stick my foot up your ass."

Jake set his end of the couch down on tailgate and hopped out of the truck bed. "I'd like to see you try it." He picked up his side and arranged it so Logan would have to go up the steps first.

Aaron came out of the house and held the door as Logan started up the stairs. "I swear, I can't leave the two of you alone for five seconds before you're sniping at each other. You revert back to being children when you get together."

"We do not!" Jake and Logan said at the same time. They looked at each other, said, "He started it," then burst out laughing.

Aaron just shook his head as they walked passed him into the house. "Yeah, there's nothing childish about either one of you. I can't see why I ever thought you were behaving like twelve-year-olds."

The exasperation in Aaron's voice was so clear it made Jake start laughing again. He and Logan chuckled as they carried the sofa into the living room and set it down facing the beige brick fireplace. Aaron replaced the cushions, while Jake stood back and surveyed the room with a clinical eye.

The couch and recliners were made of plush, dark camel suede. Aaron had chosen to use sage and chocolate as accent colors, incorporating them into the color scheme with accent pillows and an area rug. Cream-colored, silk damask curtains graced the large picture windows. Logan had handcrafted the square coffee table and end tables and had stained them in dark Peruvian walnut. The overall design was simple and homey, warm. It suited them.

Jake could well imagine them cuddled up on the sofa in front of the roaring fireplace, snuggling on a cold winter night, watching the game on Logan's big screen TV, or doing whatever it was couples did when they stayed in. A twinge of something uncomfortably close to envy skittered through Jake's brain, but he quickly squashed it. He refused to even consider that he might be jealous of his brother's boring relationship. If he had wanted that kind of thing, he could have already had it twenty times over by now. No, he preferred to be a free agent, someone who could come and go as he pleased, fuck whomever he wanted without having to answer to someone at home. The single lifestyle suited him right down to the ground. He wouldn't have it any other way.

His cell phone vibrated, catching his attention, and Jake pulled it out of his pocket to look at the caller ID. He accepted the call and shot an apologetic glance at Logan and Aaron, who stood talking quietly on the other side of the room.

"Remora here." Jake walked to the door and stood facing outside, giving himself the illusion of privacy, even as he knew every word he said was overheard. Logan was going to have to find out about this call sooner or later anyway, since they co-owned the building which housed both of their businesses.

"Mr. Remora," a nasal female voice said. "This is Janie with Sanders and Associates. I'm calling to confirm your two o'clock appointment with Mr. Sanders on Monday."

"Thank you, Janie. Please tell Mr. Sanders I'm looking forward to it. I'll be in D.C. first thing Monday morning." Jake clicked the phone closed and turned to his brother, ready for the interrogation to come.

"What was that about? You're not going all the way to D.C. for a job, are you?"

"Sort of," Jake said, hedging. "Why don't we have a seat? I need to talk to you about something."

"Okay." Logan settled on the sofa, and Aaron sat right up against his side, their shoulders rubbing. "Although, I have to tell you, nothing good has ever come from someone saying, 'I need to talk to you.' Should I be worried?"

"No. I have good news, more or less." Jake perched on the end of the chair. "I'm being headhunted by a interior design firm in Washington, D.C. called Sanders and Associates. Apparently, Sanders is related to old lady Turner. He came in for a visit and was impressed with the job I did for her last summer. Personally, I think the Heartland design was a little too suburban housewife, but he must've liked it, because he asked who did the work and contacted me."

"But… Why? Why would you want to move and work for someone else when you have your own business right here?" Aaron chirped.

"Mainly for the challenge. The money they're offering isn't half bad either. It's more than I make working on my own, that's for damn sure. I have an appointment to go in and meet the associates Monday afternoon. Get the lay of the land, so to speak, before I decide whether or not I want to accept the job offer."

"If this is about money, Jake, you know I'd be happy to help you out. I thought your finances were going well right now."

"I'm fine. I don't need your money." Jake fidgeted under Logan's brooding stare. He may have been thirty-six and fully capable of making his own decisions, but under his brother's scrutiny, he felt twelve years old. That pissed him off. He didn't need Logan's approval. Jake's life was not a damn pet project for Logan to oversee in his off-hours. The man had his own life and responsibilities to worry about and needed to keep his nose out of it. "This isn't about that. Not just that anyway."

Logan leaned forward, his elbows on his knees. "What is it about then?"

Jake took a deep breath, trying to curb the clawing urge to get defensive. "It's about business, and being able to build a bigger, better clientele. Do you have any idea the contacts I could make working in D.C.? Hell, if worse came to worst, I could always come home and reopen the shop. It isn't going anywhere. I'm not going to sell my half of the building, if that's what has your panties in a twist."

"That's not what I'm worried about, and you know it. I just don't want you to go off half-cocked and jump into something you haven't thought out. Other than Aaron, you're the only family I have left. I have a right to worry about you if I want to."

Jake felt like sticking his tongue out, but he refrained. Logan had a point, as much as it killed Jake to admit it—even if only to himself. "I appreciate your concern, bro, but I have given this some thought. And nothing is set in stone yet. I still have jobs to finish here, and I haven't even met the other associates. I'm not going to do anything rash. I promise."

"All right." Logan paused for a moment and looked at Jake as if he expected to see something other than his usual mirror image. "If this is what you want, I'm behind you."

"Thank you." Jake blew out a breath of relief. That hadn't been quite as bad as he'd imagined it. Logan could be an opinionated asshole when he set his mind to something. Although Jake didn't feel that he needed his brother's blessing, it was nice to know he'd have a soft place to land if he decided to accept the new job and everything went to pot.

Jake raised his arms and stretched, his back popping in response. "Well, I guess I'm going to head out. I have a few things I need to get done today."

"You could stay a while," Aaron said. "Hang out with us and have dinner maybe? It's the least we can do, after the help you've been with the house and all."

"It was no big deal. I think I'm just going to pick something up in town and head back to the apartment. I have some paperwork I need to wrap up. Although, I'll take you up on the free dinner if I can take a rain check."

"Sure, Jake, any time. You know you're always welcome here." Aaron and Logan rose with Jake and walked him to the door. Aaron opened it. "Oh, wait a sec. I keep meaning to tell you. That little pizza joint you like so much, Mama Celeste's, was sold the other week. Some out-of-towner bought it."

"Well, shit. Mama Celeste's was the only place left that had good, authentic brick oven pizza. Fuck."

"I stopped there last week and had lunch. Everything seems the same to me, but I'm not all that picky, like you are. I just thought you'd want to know."

"Yeah. Thanks for the heads-up." Jake said his good nights and climbed in his truck. As he headed down the road, he contemplated whether he wanted to risk ordering substandard pizza or just go home and nuke something. Laziness won out, and he decided to risk it. How bad could they possibly screw up a pizza anyway?

Chapter Three

Jake entered the pizzeria and glanced around. Much to his relief, everything looked exactly the same. Cheaply framed photos of Rome and Italy hung above twelve booths covered in red vinyl. Red and white checkered clothes covered the tabletops. An older couple ate quietly at the table closest to the door.

Further back, the same archaic jukebox that played mostly country and eighties pop music sat off to the side of the order counter and the cash register. Hanging above the counter was a menu board. Its white plastic had dulled to a dingy cream with age and announced all the house specials, including Jake's personal favorite: the fully loaded, brick oven pizza.

If Aaron hadn't told him it'd been taken over by someone new, Jake never would've guessed. He could only hope they'd maintained the recipes as well as the gaudy décor.

A delivery driver hauling an armload of red pizza warmers bumped into him as the dude hurried out the door. So much for frickin' manners. Jake frowned as he approached the counter. No one was behind it. He tapped his fingers on the laminated surface and waited.

Just when he was about to start hollering for some service, a young guy came out of the back, a harried look on his face as he wiped his hands on a dish towel. He was eye-catching, with sun-kissed skin and short, chestnut curls, although a little young and on the skinny side. Kind of cute, like a puppy you just want to take home and cuddle, though Jake's intentions wouldn't be so innocent.

The kid avoided eye contact and picked at a large red stain on the front of his shirt. "Can I help you?"

"I need to order a pizza. The brick oven, loaded, with extra cheese." Upon closer inspection, something about the other man seemed familiar to Jake, though he couldn't put his finger on why.

Was it possible he'd already fucked him? Nameless one-night stands marched through Jake's mind. No. Either I haven't fucked him or he just wasn't that memorable.

"Number?"

"Huh?" Jake locked gazes with the guy and realized he'd been so lost in thought trying to place the other man that he'd missed something. To the kid, he probably just looked like an aging geezer who'd been dozing. Maybe he'd just get his pizza and head home. Feeling old killed his libido anyway. "Sorry, I must've shorted out there for a minute. It's been a long day."

The boy gave him a tight smile. "I asked for your phone number. The computer is set up to require it. Deliveries and all, you know."

"It's okay. I know the drill." Jake rattled off his phone number and reached into his wallet, while the guy typed in his order. He dug out a credit card and then held it across the counter.

The guy shook his head, his brown curls bobbing. "I'm sorry, but we aren't set up to take them yet. We accept cash or checks though."

Jake bit his tongue as he fumbled through his wallet. They'd always accepted cards when Giuseppe owned the place.

Someone came up behind him and cleared their throat impatiently. Without turning, Jake murmured, "I'm hurrying. I'm hurrying." Damn impatient people. All he could find was a crumpled ten-dollar bill sandwiched between the receipts stuffed in his wallet. "Fuck." He glanced back at the guy behind the counter. "I don't have enough cash on me. Could you hold that thought while I run across the road to the ATM? I'll be right back."

The cashier glanced over his shoulder, presumably at the customer standing behind him, and then back to Jake. "Uh, sure."

He turned, in a rush to go get the money and get back, and rammed his shoulder into the person standing behind him. "Shit. Sorry."

"No problem," a deep male voice replied.

Instant recognition made his blood run cold.

When the familiar scent of Old Spice invaded his nostrils, Jake's brain shorted out. White noise replaced any of the thousand pithy diatribes he'd planned to say on the off chance he would ever run into this particular jackass again.

"It's been a long time, Jake. You look good."

So did he, but Jake would've rather had his eyeballs plucked out by a crow than tell the other man that. The thin, rangy frame Jake recalled from their time together had filled out in the years since they'd last seen each other. Lean muscle, apparent beneath the red polo shirt straining across the other man's chest and shoulders, and form-fitting khaki slacks were pulled taut over narrow hips and thickly muscled thighs.

All that escaped Jake's flapping mouth was the name of his ex-lover. "Kane."

"So you at least remember me then?" Kane smiled, revealing a perfect set of pearly white teeth behind his pale lips.

"Uh, yeah." Jake winced. Smooth. Real fucking smooth, Remora. Where was all his charisma when he needed it most? Thinking on his toes, Jake added, "I remember your name, Kane, but I barely recognized you. You've gotten old, man." All right, so it was a cheap shot. Jake couldn't help himself. Besides, the bastard had it coming.

Cold chills danced down Jake's spine as Kane chuckled. The throaty laugh transported him back to a time and place he didn't want to revisit, back when he was young and naive, before cold, hard reality taught him that people only used love as a convenient excuse to hurt those they claimed to care about. Love   the kind movies and novels waxed poetically about didn't exist. Lust was the only trustworthy emotion. Sex was the only constant companion Jake wanted or needed.

He'd do well to remember that while everything he'd ever dreamed of possessing stood within reach.

Kane wasn't his anymore and hadn't been for a very long time. Truth be told, he'd probably never really been Jake's to begin with. The affection they'd shared must've been a fabrication. Otherwise, things would have turned out differently. That alternate reality hadn't come to pass though, so it didn't bear thinking on. Ifs were the butter insanity thrived on.

"Fair enough." Kane's deep green gaze connected with Jake's and locked there. "So, you're still here, huh? I was wondering whether or not you were still around. How've you been?"

"I'm fine. Great, in fact. What about you?" Icy tendrils of anger and glee warred for dominance inside Jake. His stomach plummeted, and he developed a rapid case of cotton mouth. How the hell could so many emotions swirl around in his head at the same time? It seemed ludicrous that he'd be happy, but he couldn't squash the thrill he felt in response to seeing his first love again.

A good therapist would sort it out. *I'll have to make an appointment first thing Monday morning.*

"Dad?"

Kane glanced at the cute kid behind the counter. "It's okay, son. Why don't you go ahead and fix the man's pizza? I can hold down the fort up here."

Dad? Jake's attention yo-yoed from one man to the other. That would certainly explain why the kid looked so familiar.

The kid's eyes weren't green, but they were shaped the same, with up-tilting corners that had always made Kane appear as if his eyes were smiling. They shared the same golden skin tone and chestnut curls. Kane's hair was shorter now, tamed into a buzz cut. The small, round scar left by Tommy Martin's class ring when they'd fought in the tenth grade was still above the arc of Kane's left eyebrow, although it was tiny and faded by the passage of time. Kane's son hadn't inherited his father's sharp jaw or the dimple in his square chin. The boy was shorter, and skinnier, than Kane had been at sixteen, too.

Jake should know. There wasn't an inch of Kane's body that he hadn't explored at one time or another.

Of course, that felt like a lifetime ago now. Almost as if someone else had lived through those awkward years when he and Kane had been inseparable, first as friends and then as lovers. Until the plastic bubble surrounding their young love was so cruelly popped during the summer between their sophomore and junior year of high school.

Jake watched the young man walk into the back before he asked what was on the tip of his tongue. "He's yours? Your kid?"

"Yeah, he's mine." The rugged lines of Kane's face smoothed out, his eyes filling with something akin to pride. "Brock's a freshman at Tech this year."

Unsure of what to make of that, Jake just nodded. So Kane had a kid enrolled at Virginia Tech. La-ti-da. Speculation about the kid and Kane's sexual orientation ran rampant through Jake's mind.

Had his first lover decided to go straight after he'd been whisked out of town? It wasn't as if Kane had ever really come out of the closet while Jake had known him. His refusal to own up to his sexuality in the face of his parents' scorn had been the cause of Jake's heartache and, ultimately, the reason his last two years of high school had been hell on earth. Not that he still thought about what it was like to be a pariah, to be ostracized, and to be whispered about by the people he'd thought were his friends. He'd put all of that, and Kane's betrayal, behind him.

The phone rang, and the shrill sounded abnormally loud in the semi-quiet room. Brock—Jake thought that was the kid's name—hollered from the back for Kane to answer it. Kane shrugged apologetically. "Excuse me for a second."

Jake nodded more out of manners than thought. He stood transfixed, his gaze following Kane behind the counter, even as his brain screamed for him to get the hell out of Dodge. The last thing he wanted to do was hang around and talk about old times. Feeling like a pussy, Jake bolted for the door.

* * * * *

To the backdrop of Nickelback blasting from ten-inch woofers, Jake drove aimlessly for what seemed like a decade. He alternated between cursing himself for being bothered by Kane's sudden appearance in town, and railing at the man for coming back in the first place. Kane's attractive features melded and flowed from the teenager Jake had loved into the man Kane was today then back again, over and over, as if his image was made of moldable wax inside the moving picture show of Jake's head.

He saw them as boys, playing outside with the Dalmatian puppies he and Logan had received for their tenth birthday. Snapshots of the two of them camping out in a pup tent when they were twelve and skinny dipping at the river when they were fourteen revolved like a merry-go-round. Their first clumsy kiss, all lips and teeth, stood out like a beacon. Damn, he'd been terrified of making the first move and having Kane think he was a freak for wanting to kiss another boy, but he'd done it. Kane had kissed him back and more. They'd gone from kissing to touching in the blink of an eye. Those earliest fumblings had been nerve-wracking and awkward, neither

95

having the slightest knowledge of what to do, but they'd prattled along   together.

By the time Kane's mom caught them, naked and exchanging sloppy blowjobs in the basement rec room, they'd been lovers for over a year, having sex whenever and wherever they could steal a spare minute alone together. All of it ended when Kane's mother walked in on them.

The front driver side tire hit a pothole in the road and bounced the cab, jarring Jake's teeth. They snapped down on his tongue, sinking into the flesh, and the coppery tang of blood filled his mouth.

Fuck. This day can't get any shittier.

He'd been planning to eat, catch up on the paperwork he'd brought home, and then go out for a little fun. Maybe hit a nightclub or two, see what kind of entertainment he could find. Instead, he was wallowing in memories he'd rather forget and was feeling sorry for himself like the jackass Logan always claimed he was.

Logan. That fucker.

Jake felt around on the seat until his fingers closed around his cell phone. He picked it up and hit the speed dial, calling his brother to give him a piece of his mind.

He waited for Logan to say hello before tearing in on him. "You know, you could have at least warned me, you meddling asshole. How could you let me walk in there without knowing what I was getting myself into?"

"Huh? I don't know what you're going on about, Jake."

"Don't play stupid with me." Jake shouldered the cell phone and hit his turn signal, making a left toward home. "You and Aaron are the ones who told me Mama Celeste's had been bought out."

"Um… Actually, it was Aaron who told you that, not me. I haven't been in there since it was sold. What does that have to do with anything? One of your throwaway boy-toys have his new daddy buy it for him or something?"

"As if I would be pissed off about that." Jake snorted. "Kane fuckin' Sharp bought it."

"What? You can't be serious. Kane's back in town?"

Jake believed the shock he heard in his brother's voice. Maybe he hadn't known after all. "Oh, yeah. He's moved home, with his son the Tech student in tow. There's probably a Mrs. Sharp hiding in the woodwork too. I'm sure the kid wasn't hatched from a fucking egg." Jake swerved into the parking lot in front of his apartment complex and cut the engine.

"Well, yeah, but…Jesus." Aaron's voice echoed in the background, asking Logan what was going on.

"Tell me about it. You weren't the one forced to make small talk with him in public." Jake exited the truck and started inside while he listened to Logan tell Aaron they would talk about it after he got off the phone.

"Damn," Logan said. "Did Kane say anything about what happened?"

"No. What exactly would he have said? 'Sorry I accused you of trying to rape me. It was all just a big misunderstanding.'"

"I don't think that would've gone over too well."

"Yeah, me neither." Jake unlocked the door to his first floor apartment and stepped inside. "What did you expect him to say?"

"I don't know. How about 'I'm sorry'? That would pretty much cover it."

"An apology doesn't mean much twenty years after the fact."

Logan was quiet, as if he were carefully choosing his next words, while Jake flipped on the light switch inside the door. Finally, he said, "Shit, Jake, he was just a kid. You both were."

Jake swallowed the urge to scream as he stomped into the kitchen. "Fuck you, Logan. You didn't go through all the hell I had to deal with."

"No, but I was there. I know exactly how bad things got for you. It's time to let it go."

"I have." Jake plucked a crystal decanter off the sidebar between the living room and kitchen and poured himself four fingers of Crown Royal. He turned the glass up to his lips and swallowed, hissing as the liquor burned a path to his stomach and hit like a lead weight.

"If that's true, then why are you drinking? Don't think I'm stupid enough to believe that's soda you're guzzling."

Jake slammed the empty glass down on the bar and poured himself another drink. "Think you're smart, don't you?"

"Why do you even care that he's here?"

"I don't," Jake huffed. "I just didn't like being surprised with it."

"Well, it's not like you aren't planning to move soon anyway."

"That isn't concrete yet. I already told you   I have to go out there and meet the rest of the staff and shit first."

"Whatever. If you weren't set on it, you wouldn't have mentioned it at all."

"That's bullshit. I just wanted you to know, in case I decide to take the job offer. I didn't want to throw it at you out of the blue." Although, accepting the job is looking better with every breath.

"I have another call coming in," Logan said. "Hang on a minute."

"All ri—" Jake was cut off mid-word. Dead air echoed in his ears as he poured himself another drink, guzzled it down, and waited. Finally, he got tired of being on hold and hung up. The least his brother could have done was pop back over and tell him he had to go instead of leaving him hanging.

Asshole.

Chapter Four

Jake stepped into the shower, closed his eyes, and tilted his face up toward the scalding spray of water, letting it cascade down over his skull. He wet his hair and blindly reached for shampoo, then lathered and rinsed himself free of the sudsy foam. His face and body was next. The scent of vanilla filled the humid air as he soaped up, working his way from top to bottom.

At some point while he scrubbed, his dick decided to take a liking to the tactile sensations of hot water and his hands roaming his skin. Being Saturday night—and over a week since he'd gotten laid—his balls weren't too choosy about who fulfilled their desires.

He wrapped a soapy hand around his shaft and gave it a good, firm pump from base to tip, working his foreskin back and forth over the sensitive crown. Pleasurable tingles radiated from his dick, prompting him to repeat the caress again. And again.

Glancing down, he watched his cock slide through the snug tunnel of his fist, the rounded tip appearing with every downward pull. Clear pearls of desire lubricated the taut sheath of his foreskin and dripped from his slit, only to be quickly washed away by the shower's mist. With a tight grip, he stroked harder. Tension coiled in his groin as his balls inched closer to his pelvis. Through the slick fist sliding up and down his shaft, he could feel his pulse echo through his shaft and gain momentum, racing toward the finish. He stroked faster, his attention centered on the uppermost inches of his cock.

Mmm, just a little more.

The sound of ringing bells filled the air, though muted through by the thick glass of the shower door.

"Fuck." Jake twirled around underneath the water and quickly rinsed off. He was damn tempted to ignore the doorbell   and Logan, who was probably pacing out in the hall while he waited. He grabbed a towel from the rack and hastily scrubbed his skin dry as made his way through the apartment, leaving a trail of wet footprints on the hardwood floor in his wake.

After knotting the white towel around his hips, Jake pulled open the door. "What do you—? Oh…"

Evening air raced across his body, chilling his skin and causing an avalanche of goose bumps. He stared at Kane, flabbergasted to find the man standing outside his home, wearing a cocky grin and holding a large white and red pizza box.

What the hell is he doing here?

Not bothering to disguise his interest, Kane looked Jake up and down. "If this is how you greet all your visitors, I'll have to come by more often."

"You think so?"

"Definitely." Kane sauntered past Jake and into the apartment, brushing up against him as he walked by.

"By all means, come on in." Jake flicked his wrist, and the door shut with a thud. He turned and watched Kane set the pizza box down on one of the black stools in front of the bar. "Make yourself at home."

"Thanks."

"I was being sarcastic, asshole."

Kane propped his hip against the bar. "I know."

"What are you doing here, Kane?" Jake edged closer, conscious of being practically naked in front of his old lover. He was proud of his body, and under normal conditions, he didn't mind flaunting it, but it wasn't the figure he'd had at sixteen. As much as he worked out, it never would be again. Growing old was hell on a gay man's self-image.

"You forgot your pizza. I had to wait until the restaurant closed—we're too short-staffed for me to leave earlier—but I brought it to you."

"Uh-huh. That may be a decent excuse for the start of a porno, but I'm not buying it. What do you want, Kane?" Jake finger combed his wet hair, pushing it away from his face. Water dripped from the curling ends and trickled down his back in itchy rivulets, further dampening the towel around his ass.

"Cutting right to the chase, huh? Okay, I can do that." Kane ran his hand over his lower face, a mannerism Jake recognized as something he only did when nervous. "I wanted to tell you how much I regret the things that happened when we were kids. I can't tell you how much I've thought about that day over the years and wished I could change it. I know it's probably a case of too little, too late, but I'd really like it if you could forgive me."

Not fucking likely. "No problem. It was a long time ago."

"Great." Kane shot him a tremulous smile. "Maybe now that I'm back in town, we could hang out some time. Catch up on old times and stuff."

"Yeah, sure." So not going to happen. "As long as we can, uh, both work it into our schedules."

"Of course. Things are crazy at the restaurant right now, but I'm sure it'll improve once I can get a few more reliable people hired. So, um, what do you do now? For a living, I mean. I remember how you used to talk about moving to Europe and painting. Being the next Picasso."

Jake rested his ass on one of the two barstools and sighed. Small talk was going to be the death of him. "The painting thing didn't work out. I had big aspirations and little actual talent, or so my college art instructor said. I work in interior design now."

"That's cool."

"Yeah. It's all right. So, uh…" Jake searched for something to say. Frankly, he had a lot of questions, but he wasn't entirely sure he wanted to know the answers. Part of him wanted to ask how Kane knew where he lived, but it didn't take a genius to figure it out. Blacksburg was a small town, and he was listed in the phone book. Hell, Kane only needed to look as far as his own pizza delivery database.

Kane's kid and the whole gay/not gay thing crowded into the forefront of his mind, but he didn't want to touch that subject right now. He felt like he was treading on eggshells as it was. "How did you end up Mama Celeste's? I didn't even know it was for sale. No one thought Giuseppe would ever retire. He has to be pushing seventy by now."

"Well," Kane said as he settled back against the wall, "believe it or not, my parents kept in contact with a few people from here after we moved. When my mother passed away last year, Giuseppe came to her funeral. We talked afterward, and he mentioned that he wanted to retire but couldn't really afford to close the restaurant unless he had a buyer, someone he could trust to keep the pizzeria open and not ruin what he'd spent his life working to build. Since Brock had already been accepted to Tech, it seemed like fate's way of stepping in and pointing out what I should do. I'm not sure he likes that his old man followed him here, but it does make it more convenient for him to bum money off of me."

"I'm sorry to hear about your mom."

"Hey, it's okay. I miss her, but she was ready to join Dad."

"Your dad's gone too, then?"

"Yeah. Lung cancer took him a little over five years ago. What about your folks?"

"Gone. They were in a car wreck not long after Logan and I graduated high school."

"I'm sorry. That must have been rough."

"Yeah, but it was a long time ago."

Awkward silence stretched between them. Jake fiddled with the towel around his hips and wondered if it would be rude to ask Kane to leave, so he could get dressed. Of course, if Kane left, there wouldn't really be any need to cover up anyway.

Kane stuck his hands in the pockets and rocked back on his heels, drawing Jake's attention to the bulge straining against the front of his pants. A package that looked quite a bit larger than Jake remembered. Remnants of his earlier desire crashed over him and made his dick to lurch and swell beneath the plush bath towel around his hips. He licked his lips, hungry for a taste of what the other man was hiding inside his Dockers.

He briefly considered making a move, until he looked up and met Kane's eyes. Something flashed through Kane's eyes and echoed inside Jake—a static charge of old lust and the vestige of warm affection.

Things had ended shitty between them. Worse, he realized, was how his emotions for the other man had been trapped inside him, forced down by anger and never truly dealt with. He'd gone from being over the moon in love to being cast straight into the bowels of hell with no go-between, no closure to speak of.

Would it be such a bad idea to come onto him? Just fuck Kane and be done with it. Possibly get the man out of his system once and for all. Sex wasn't a cure-all—he knew that—but it was real and tangible, and something Jake was good at.

Surely, the chemistry they shared was nothing more than physical attraction. The pull he felt toward Kane was probably only a figment of Jake's overactive imagination. A mere response from having seen someone who'd haunted him for twenty years. It had to be. No one else had lasted beyond one fuck with him. He was confident Kane wouldn't be any different. Sex would clear the cobwebs of his memory and would expose his feelings as nothing more than nostalgia. He didn't want to feel anything for Kane. Not attraction, not hatred, not love. Absolutely nothing.

Jake stood, his arms hanging at his sides, and let his towel drop to the floor. "Whoops."

Kane's eyes rounded and then he bent at the waist, his gaze on the floor. "I'll get it." He plucked the towel off the floor and glanced up, his face level with Jake's groin. "Uh…here." He held up the towel and slowly straightened, his lean cheeks tinged with pink.

Jake accepted the cloth and wrapped it low around his hips, leaving the knot loose, the fabric gaping open over one thigh. "Thanks."

Kane swallowed, his Adam's apple bobbing. "No problem."

They stood a foot apart, gazes locked. Kane's chest rose and fell, taxing the snug fit of his polo shirt. Jake could smell him; a hint of Old Spice cologne and the musky aroma of a hard day's work. A five o'clock shadow covered Kane's jaw, the stubble only adding a roguish allure to his boy-next-door good looks. The way he looked at Jake—the heat in his eyes, his dilated pupils—was enough to entice Jake into taking a single step forward, closing the space between them.

He didn't give himself a moment to rethink what he was doing or about the possible consequences. Right or wrong, he wanted Kane, and he was going to have him.

Jake crowded Kane against the bar and covered the other man's lips with his. Kane gasped, his mouth pliable but unmoving under Jake's. Just when he was sure Kane would push him away, Jake felt the other man's hands land on his shoulders. Fingers rubbed over Jake's skin as Kane's lips parted.

Kane pulled Jake closer and deepened the kiss, sucking on Jake's tongue like it was the sweetest thing he'd ever tasted. A deep moan escaped Jake, surprising him. He was not a moaner and certainly not from something as simple as a kiss. Kane nibbled Jake's lower lip, sucking on it, and his brain shorted out, no longer concerned about whether or not he'd made a peep.

One long kiss melted into another, their mouths moving in concert until Jake didn't know which way was up. His heart galloped like an overworked field horse, and his dick ached, full to bursting with need. Kane tasted so good, a mix of salt and something sweeter, almost minty. It was the opposite of the cinnamon and spice flavor of the Big Red chewing gum Kane had favored in high school. The man's soft, malleable tongue was like a mini cyclone as Kane licked over Jake's teeth and explored the recesses of his mouth. He withdrew and taunted Jake to give chase with his own.

Kane's fingers kneaded Jake's shoulders, massaging muscles he hadn't even realized were tight with stress. The tension fell away with a flex of Kane's nimble fingers. A lesser man would've melted into a relaxed pile of goo at Kane's feet, but that wasn't the impression Jake wanted to leave with his former lover. No, he wanted to stun Kane and leave the man begging for more, not the other way around.

In an attempt to turn things around, Jake grabbed Kane by the upper arms, whirled him around, and backed him toward the sofa. It was closer than the bedroom, only a few feet away, and plenty wide enough to suit his purposes. Surely, Kane must've realized his intentions, but the other man didn't break their kiss or resist, leading Jake to believe they shared the same ultimate goal—*sex*.

After what felt like a millennia but couldn't have been more than thirty seconds, the back of Kane's legs finally ran into the arm of the couch. Jake gave Kane a light shove, pushed the man down on the couch, and then crawled on top of him. The towel snagged on something—whether the couch or Kane's belt, Jake didn't know or care—and was quickly forgotten as he straddled Kane's narrow hips.

He looked down at Kane and saw the features of the boy he'd once loved shining out through the older man's face. The roundness of youth was gone, replaced by sharp planes and angles. Tiny laugh lines radiated out from the corners of Kane's eyes, hinting at all the years and experiences they hadn't shared. Instead of being angry or disheartened at that thought, Jake wondered about what he'd missed out on, curious about all the intricate details that had shaped Kane into the man he'd become. However, he was smart enough not to ask. Questions would kill the mood. Knowing where Kane had been wasn't pertinent to what they were about to do. They didn't need to know each other's life history in order to fuck. The fact that he'd never so much as wondered about any of his other lovers' histories didn't even occur to him.

Kane wrapped a hand around Jake's neck and pulled him down for a kiss. Even as their lips smacked together, mouths open for more, Jake slid his hand between them and reached for Kane's belt. As sexy as it felt to bare-assed naked while Kane was completely dressed, he wanted more skin, needed to see and feel everything Kane had to offer.

His fingers fumbled with the buckle, clumsy as Kane's tongue entered his mouth and danced against his own. When it gave way, he felt like cheering. Only a button and zipper stood in the way of his reaching Kane's cock, something he desperately wanted to see and touch.

God, how many times had they done this—made out on a sofa, before or after school, on the weekends while their parents were at church? They were men now, but being with Kane still made Jake feel like a green youth. His balls ached and churned, ready to fire, as his body screamed for more. More skin, more physical contact.

Blindly, he popped the button Kane's pants and slid the zipper down. Sticking his hand through the open flap, Jake reached into Kane's pants.

Kane pulled his mouth away, his breath coming in choppy pants. "Wait." He placed a hand against the center of Jake's chest and pushed. "Stop."

Jake blinked down at him, confused. "Why?"

105

"One minute you seemed pissed to see me, and the next, you're all over me. I need to know why you're doing this."

"Um, to come. Does there need to be a more important reason?"

"Yes."

"Shit." Jake sighed and sat up. "I don't know. You're hot. You're here. What the hell do you want from me?"

Kane moved away from him, sitting on the far side of the sofa. "I don't know. A little honesty would be nice."

Jake sneered, his ire rising fast. "Who do you think you are, talking to me about honesty? What a crock."

"I didn't show up here for a quick fuck, Jake. I came because it was nice seeing you—brought back a lot of good memories—and I thought maybe we could work things out and be friends again." Kane ran a hand over the stubble on his head. "I guess that was a foolish idea."

The crestfallen look on Kane's face sliced into Jake's conscience, which only served to piss him off more. "Am I supposed to apologize now and promise we'll be best friends forever? Grow up. What we had was spe—" Jake clicked his tongue and started over, quickly rephrasing his words to keep from admitting too much. "What we had is over. You made sure of that. You're the one who showed up here tonight of your own volition and started making googly eyes at me. If you want to screw, I can accommodate you. Anything else is out of the question."

Kane's forehead wrinkled, and his mossy green eyes narrowed into slits beneath lowered chestnut brows. "Fuck you."

"I thought we just established that wasn't going to happen. Either you want it or you don't." Jake moved in closer, crowding Kane against the arm of the sofa, and cupped his cock through the material of his pants and squeezed. "Which is it?"

Kane shoved Jake, pushing him away. "Who are you? You're not the person I remember."

"Sorry to disappoint you, lover," Jake sneered. "Some of us had to grow up."

"Apparently not for the better." Kane shook his head and looked at Jake as if he was something hanging off the bottom of his shoe. "What happened to you? You used to be so easy to talk to, always smiling and happy."

"Life happened to me." Jake cleared his throat, trying to get rid of the sudden lump of emotion blocking his windpipe. "Only an idiot runs around happy-go-lucky all the time." He scooped the towel up off the floor and hastened to secure it around his waist as he hustled the few steps to the door and pulled it open.

"Who the hell are you to judge me anyway? You're the little boy who cried rape and ran away to wherever the fuck you've been for the last two decades. I'm the one who was left behind to live in the shadow of your lie. Not only a queer, but a deviant one, who took advantage of poor, little straight boys when they least expected it. Do you think anyone would have a damn thing to do with me after you left? It doesn't matter that your parents didn't press charges. The way they whisked you out of town was enough proof as far as everyone else was concerned. I was guilty, regardless of what really happened."

"That was twenty years ago, Jake. I'm sorry I said what I did, but I was young and stupid, afraid of being disowned if my parents found out. If I could, I would happily go back and change what happened, but that just isn't possible. You need to get over it and move on."

"Yeah, well, that's easy for you to say."

With an intent look, Kane stared at Jake, giving him the disturbing notion that the other man saw right into the depths of his soul and somehow found him lacking. Jake tore his gaze away, unwilling to continue this conversation into the insanity it offered and fixed his attention on the doorframe.

Kane walked passed Jake, stopped just outside the door, and looked back over his shoulder. "I..." His voice faded as he turned away and continued down the hallway. Whatever he'd planned to say hung unfinished in the air as he disappeared around the corner.

Jake slammed the door and headed toward the bar, intent on finishing what he'd started earlier. The shower and his little tête-à-tête with Kane had more than killed his buzz. Maybe the alcohol would take care of his hard-on, along with the droning ache behind his eyes. His brain hurt from overanalyzing things. The fog of being drunk held plenty of appeal—for several different reasons.

Chapter Five

After a grueling day of self-imposed paperwork and chores around the house to keep his mind off Kane and his impending job interview, Jake showered and cleaned himself up. He dressed in his favorite leather pants and a tight black T-shirt, and hauled ass out of the house for a little fun. There weren't really any gay bars in Blacksburg, per se, but most of the clubs were college oriented and laid back, a melting pot of sexualities and cultures. He figured he would have a few drinks, see what was going on, maybe find someone to play with until he was ready to call it a night. Even if nothing came from it—and that was a rarity—the drunken collegiate eye candy was always entertaining.

He was sitting at the bar at Reinfield's, halfway through his second beer, when all hell broke loose. A girl's scream filled the air, the high pitch of her voice almost loud enough to shatter ears drums. Jake swiveled on his stool in time to see a big bruiser push a blonde girl—presumably the one who'd been yelling bloody murder—behind him and launch across the table toward a smaller guy, who had his back toward the crowd. The young guy jumped out of his chair, narrowly missing the jock's outstretched hands as he backpedaled. His quick thinking came at a price though, as he seemed to trip over his own feet and began to fall backward, his arms windmilling wildly.

Jake winced as the other man plummeted to the floor and landed on his ass. Damn, that had to hurt his pride.

As if being embarrassed in front of his peers wasn't enough punishment for whatever transgression the kid had committed, the jock smacked the lightweight table out of his way—knocking it over and splashing the drinks atop it all over the couple sitting nearby—and kept coming toward the youth.

The kid climbed to his feet and backed away from his nemesis, drawing closer to the bar. The nearer he came, the more Jake could make out what was being said.

"I'm sorry. I didn't know she was your girlfriend," the boy pleaded.

"You should have thought of that before you hit on my girl and poured your drink all over her, jackass."

"That was an accident! It wouldn't have happened, if you hadn't pushed me."

"What are you saying? That it's my fault you ruined her favorite top?"

"No." The kid held his hands up in front of him. "No, that isn't what I meant at all. I was just saying it wasn't entirely my fault either. Please. Stop. You don't want to do this."

"Oh, I don't, huh? I think I do. Someone needs to teach you little Tech punks a lesson. You move to town and think you're better than everyone else, just 'cause we don't go to your fancy college. Well, pretty boy, we'll see just how special you are when I'm kicking your ass."

The boy ran into a barstool someone had left sitting out and knocked it over with a crash. He glanced around wildly, his neck swiveling like it was made of rubber. His eyes were as wide as saucers, almost pleading for someone to intervene on his behalf.

It was then that Jake got a good glimpse of the kid's face and realized who was about to get his ass stomped—Brock.

He set down his beer, torn between helping the kid out and ignoring the skirmish. It really wasn't any of his business. Besides, he rationalized, if the kid was wily enough to wrangle his way into an over-twenty-one club while being under the legal age to drink in Virginia, then he could surely get his ass out in one piece.

Brock swung at the bigger man and missed his face by a foot, his fist barely glancing off the other guy's shoulder. The energy behind the kid's swing propelled him around in a semicircle, leaving his back unguarded to his opponent.

Jake swore. Apparently, the little shit wasn't very smart at all.

Movement from behind the bar caught Jake's attention. He turned to see the bartender waving at someone through the crowd, no doubt signaling for the doorman to come in and help bust up the fight.

With a sigh, Jake rose to his feet. He ought to let the kid take his whippin' and go the hell home before the police were called. It would serve Brock right for sneaking into a club when he should have had his ass at home, where he belonged. That's exactly what Jake would've let happen, if he thought his conscience would cut him a little slack. Since that wasn't going to happen, he headed toward the end of the bar and Brock.

The jock shoved Brock from behind, planting him face first on the ground. The big guy reared back his leg, readying for a kick, when Jake forced his way between them. He shot the jock a menacing look. "Back off."

"Why don't you mind your own business, Grandpa?"

Grandpa, my ass. "I said, back the fuck off, kid." Jake kept his gaze on the jock and held his ground, waiting for the other man to retreat. He knew better than to turn his back on an intoxicated man. The term "fair fight" was not synonymous with "drunken brawl."

Even though Jake towered close to four inches above the jock's six-foot height, the other man seemed undaunted. He got right up in Jake's face and sneered, the smell of Jäger strong on his breath. "What, you deaf or somethin'? Forget your hearin' aid, old man?"

The crowd tittered, the air filling with malevolence. The drunken idiots were spoiling for a fight. Jake took a deep breath and let it out, trying to keep his cool. "Listen, buddy "

The man raised his hand and gave Jake a shove. "I'm not your fucking buddy, loser."

Jake stumbled back a step before quickly righting his balance, grateful he hadn't drunk more. A few more beers and he probably would have spun ass over teakettle and ended up on the floor beside Brock. A spike of adrenaline kicked in, rush-

110

ing through Jake's veins as he turned to face the punk who'd shoved him. "All right, you little fucker, that's about all the bullshit "

As his head turned, Jake's face collided with the punk's fist. Pain exploded through his head as hard-ass knuckles cut into his left cheekbone, making his eye feel like it was going to pop out of his head and yo-yo back and forth like a damned cartoon.

Fuck. That hurt.

Jake growled, fisting his hands. He jerked his arm back for momentum and slammed the punk in the nose. The younger man howled and backed off, his hands flying to his face as blood spurted from his nostrils and sprayed down the front of his shirt.

"Guess that'll teach you to fuck with Grandpa, kid." Jake shook out his hand, his knuckles stinging, and spun around to look for Brock.

Kane's boy was standing behind him, already on his feet. "Damn, I guess you showed him. Asshole."

"Yeah, well…" Out of the corner of his eye, Jake saw Reinfield's bouncer making his way through the crowd. Jake grabbed Brock's arm and gave it a tug. "Come on, kid. We need to get out of here."

"But why? He isn't going to be any more trouble. Man, I think you broke his fucking nose the way it was bleeding."

"The bouncer's coming, you little idiot. You want to get caught in here with no ID? I don't think your dad would care for having to bail your skinny ass out of jail tonight."

"Hey, it's cool. I have a fake one. That's how I got in."

Jake tightened his grip on Brock's forearm and dragged him through the club, heading for the back exit. "It's not cool, kid. Your fake ID might stand up to the doorman's scrutiny, but I don't think the cops are going to buy that you're a day over eighteen. I don't care how good it is."

Pushing open the emergency exit, Jake pulled Brock outside and slammed the door shut behind them. He let go of the kid's arm and started down the narrow alley between Reinfield's and the brick building next door, figuring his job was over. He'd done his Good Samaritan bit for the night and kept the boy out of trouble; how Brock made it home was his own problem.

To Jake's consternation, the kid tagged along behind him. Jake sped up his pace, anxious to get back to his truck, parallel parked in front of the club on Main Street.

"Hey, wait up." Brock's footsteps were loud on the damp pavement, like a puppy's exuberant hopping. "The least you could do is give me a ride home, dude. You're the one who made me leave, and my ride's still inside."

Jake kept going. Over his shoulder, he said, "The least I could've done is let you get your ass beat and gone home without having been punched in the face by your little friend back there."

"Oh, come on, man. I really need a lift."

"Call a cab." The last thing Jake wanted to do was pay a late night visit to Kane's house. He'd rather have a root canal with no anesthesia.

"I don't have any cash. Besides, do you know how hard it is to get a cab around here? It's not like back at home, where all you had to do was throw out your arm and hail one. You actually have to call for a cab here. God knows how long I'd have to wait before one showed up."

The exasperation in the kid's voice was almost funny. Curiosity got the better of Jake. "Where exactly was home for you, Brock? Before the move, I mean."

"NYC, born and raised."

"Oh." Jake exited the alley and hit the sidewalk at a fast clip. Didn't it just figure that Kane's parents would move him to a big city like New York? As if that was going to get him away from the taint of bad influences they'd classified as anyone other than straight, white bread Christians.

"Shouldn't you know that already? I thought you were friends with my dad."

Jake bit his tongue, stilling the smartass comment he wanted to make and said, "Yeah, sort of."

"What does that mean, sort of? Either you are, or you aren't."

"Jesus, you're a nosy little shit. Didn't anyone ever tell you that curiosity killed the cat?"

"Well, yeah, Dad says that all the time, but I figure if I don't ask, then I'm never going to learn what I want to know. So, are you or aren't you friends with my dad?"

Reaching his truck, Jake pulled out his keys and hit the wireless remote to unlock the doors. "None of your business, kid."

"My name isn't kid, you know? It's Brock. What's yours, by the way?"

"Jake."

"Jake what?" Brock opened the passenger side door and climbed in.

Jake gritted his teeth and got in his truck, slamming the door closed behind him. It looked like he was taking the kid home after all. "Remora."

"Oh, shit. I know who you are. You're the Antichrist."

Jake's jaw clenched. "Excuse me?"

"I remember hearing my grandma and Dad talk about you. You're the guy who corrupted Dad and forced them to move when he was a teenager. Holy shit!"

Jake glanced over at the kid and found him grinning. "You think that's funny, do you? How would you like it if someone ran around claiming you were the spawn of Satan?"

"People can think what they want. I don't give a shit."

"Just sit over there and shut up." Jake started up the engine and pulled out onto the road. Once he was headed toward his apartment, he realized he wasn't going home and didn't have the first clue where Kane lived. "Uh, where am I taking you?"

"Thought you wanted me to shut up."

"I can stop the truck and drop your ass off right here, if that's the way you want to play it, kid." He'd had about enough of the smart-aleck routine. God, why did people even want to have children if they were all lippy like this one?

"All right, chill out a little. I was just teasing. Jesus. I live on the corner of Eighth and Graham. Dad says it's the old McPherson place, although I have no damn idea who the hell McPherson is. Know which one I'm talking about?"

"Yeah, I know the house you're talking about." As well he should, since he and Kane had often spent the night there growing up.

They'd gone to school with Jeb McPherson and bunked over at his house on more than one occasion, since Jeb's parents never seemed to be home. With free run of the house, the three of them had gotten into all kinds of shit together. It was where they'd drunk their first beer and had raided Jeb's father's study for his collection of hetero porn. Watching all those bouncing tits on the television was when Jake first realized he'd rather watch his buddies jerk off than the naked girls on screen. Jeb was one first to ostracize him after the rumors about he and Kane began to circulate. His parents had put the house up for sale and relocated to Florida a few years earlier.

Thinking about Kane living there now, instead of the house he'd grown up in, was weird, although Jake supposed he had to live somewhere.

Thankfully, the rest of the short drive was silent. Jake pulled up in front of the small, white house and put his truck in park. "Well, here you are. Home sweet home."

"Yeah, thanks for the ride." Brock opened the door, causing the interior light to pop on, and hopped out. Standing in the opening between the cab and door, Brock glanced over his shoulder at Jake. "What? You're not coming in?"

"Why would I do that?" Or even want to? He was going home, hitting the sack for a good night's sleep, and leaving first thing in the morning for D.C. End of story.

"I just thought you might want to say hi to Dad or something. I'm sure he'd want to thank you for giving me a lift."

There was an odd gleam in the kid's eye that made Jake nervous. Almost like he was up to something. "That's quite all right, thanks." You can shut the door and go away now.

For all he knew, Kane and the kid's mother were cozied up inside, waiting on their sole offspring to get home. After Kane's visit to his apartment, Jake didn't want to believe there was anyone else involved in the man's life, but it was possible. Just because he had a hard time picturing Kane being unfaithful didn't mean it couldn't happen. People cheated all the time;

114

it was a fact of life. This only served to make Jake feel cheap, like some hidden secret out of a gothic novel.

An image of Kane in bed with a woman, someone who possessed Brock's brown eyes and a curvy version of the boy's petite bone structure, flashed through Jake's mind. The couple huddled together under white silk sheets, their bodies entwined as they exchanged slow, deep kisses.

Jake's chest tightened, and he quickly banished the image, mentally scrubbing the picture away. Why did he keep torturing himself with these useless thoughts? Since when was he such a fucking masochist?

"Well," Jake said, with a touch of irritation. "Are you going to go in the house or not, kid?"

"Yes. I just...shit." Brock bit into his lower lip and fidgeted. "Listen, I think I know who you are. To Dad, I mean. He doesn't talk about you, but I've seen the photo album he keeps in his bedroom closet. The one he doesn't think I know about."

"You mean you saw..." Jake's words faded as the implications of what Brock was saying hit home with the force of a sledgehammer. Surely Kane hadn't hung onto the Instamatic photos they'd taken of each other so long ago. Hell, Jake hadn't even thought of those pictures in ages.

They'd thought they were such big shits, using his mother's instant camera to snap photos of each other in all manner of racy poses. They hadn't been brave enough to take any scandalous pictures of the two of them together, but the ones they had taken said plenty about their relationship if anyone took the time to read between the lines. No teenager would pose like that with someone who was just a friend.

Brock had the good grace to look bashful. "A few years ago, when I was fifteen, I got bored and decided to be nosy and go through Dad's things. I found a locked box in the bottom of his closet. It didn't take a genius to figure out the combination. Dad uses the same two passwords for everything, either his birthday or mine. Anyway, I found the album and an old class ring inside the box."

"Mine?"

"Yeah." Brock nodded. "Your initials are engraved on the side of the band."

"Damn, I always thought I'd lost it." He'd never cared much for jewelry and had hardly worn the thing. It'd dangled on a chain from his bedroom mirror for the longest time. He hadn't even noticed it was missing until six months after Kane had left.

"Nope. Dad has it. And those pictures…" Brock waggled his eyebrows. "Those are some crazy-ass things the two of you were doing. Although, I have to admit, I skipped over the ones of Dad naked, because that's just gross."

Jake laughed. "Gross, huh?" The last thing Jake would've described Kane as was gross, now or then. The man was as hot and sweet as spun sugar. Jake had thought he hung the moon, for a while anyway.

"Uh…yeah. He is my dad, for Christ's sake. Would you want to see your old man naked?"

Jake shuddered. "No, definitely not."

"That's what I thought."

"Does Kane know you went snooping through his stuff and found those things?"

"God, no. I'm not an idiot. Dad would've killed me. Hell, he's never even really came right out and told me he's gay, but I'm not stupid. He's never had women over or gone out on dates, like most single parents. Even before I found the pictures, I figured he was either gay or a monk."

Isn't that just curious. "What about your mother?"

"Oh. Well, she's never been around. I've met her once, when I was little, but that's about it. Dad says she's not a bad person. She was just really young and not ready for kids when I came along." He shrugged. "It happens, I guess."

There was probably a hell of a lot more to that story than the kid was sharing, but Jake couldn't blame him for not going on and on about it. It wasn't as if Brock really knew him, which actually brought up a pretty damn good question or two. "Exactly what's the purpose of telling me all this, Brock?"

"From the pictures, I figure you and my dad had a thing when you were young. Then he moved away and that ended,

116

right? So, there's no reason why you couldn't start things back up now that he's here again." Brock's head tilted, his chin jutting out. "I mean, you seem to be single, otherwise you wouldn't be out clubbing. He's new in town, sort of, and kind of lonely. So…how about it? What do you think?"

Jesus Christ and all the freaking apostles. The kid was actually trying to be a matchmaker.

It would almost be cute, if the boy was trying to ply his wares on someone else. "I think you need to mind your own business, and let your dad find his own dates."

"Well, I had to try." Brock shrugged.

"Whatever, kid. Now how about you shut my door and get your butt in the house already. I have things to do that don't include talking to you about stuff that's beyond your understanding." Like putting a steak on his face in the hopes that it wouldn't swell up and make him look like a hooligan for his job interview. Maybe jerking off before he went to sleep.

Brock was saved from answering when the porch light blazed to life. Before Jake could exhale, the front door opened and Kane appeared silhouetted in the doorway, dressed in a pair of low-slung, blue gym shorts and nothing more. "Brock? Is that you out there?"

"Yeah, Dad. It's just me." Brock grinned at Jake. "And Jake."

Little bastard. "I am so going to stick my foot up your ass, kid."

Brock snickered. "Sounds kinky. Have I mentioned I'm straight?"

"Smartass," Jake growled.

"Jake?" Kane asked, stepping out onto the porch.

With a groan, Jake rolled down his window and turned off the truck. "Hey, Kane. Nice night, isn't it?" Okay, so that made him sound slightly slow-witted, but what the hell was he supposed to say? Hi Kane. Sorry I'm here, but I had to give your boy a lift home after I saved him from getting his ass kicked. That didn't have a nice ring to it.

Kane approached the truck slowly, like he was afraid Jake was going to start it up and run him over. "Uh, I guess."

Brock finally shut the damn door, pitching the cab into darkness, and walked around the front of it. He stopped at the edge of the paved driveway and waved. "I'm going to hit the bed. Thanks for the lift home, Jake. See you around."

Chapter Six

Kane waited until the door closed behind Brock before he rounded on Jake. "What in hell are you doing with my son? If this is some sick trick to get back at me, you can save yourself the trouble. Brock isn't gay."

Jake bit into the inside of his cheek to keep from laughing. Kane looked damn cute when he was pissed off   his face flushed, and his vibrant green eyes flashed. If Jake hadn't already been punched once that night, he probably would have told Kane as much, but he didn't think his face could take a second bashing. He was probably going to look a sight in the morning as it was. "I may be a lot of things, Kane, but I'm not a rapist or into jailbait, so just calm your ass down. I only gave the kid a ride home."

"For fuck's sake, don't you think that horse has been beat enough?"

A heartbeat passed before Jake figured out what he'd said and how Kane must've taken it. "I didn't mean it like that, okay."

Kane sighed and lifted his arm, running his palms over the top of his head. "I'm sorry. I guess I'm a little touchy tonight. What were you doing out with Brock?"

With his gaze locked on the shift and play of Kane's pecs and abdomen as the other man stretched, it took Jake a moment to register the question. "I ran into him at Reinfield's and gave him a lift home. It's no big deal."

Kane stepped closer to the truck. He scrutinized Jake's face for a moment before reaching out with one hand to skim his fingers a hairbreadth away from the swollen skin under Jake's eye. "It doesn't look like nothing. Brock didn't do this, did he?"

118

Jake snorted. "Not likely. The guy who wanted to rearrange Brock's face for hitting on his girl did it."

"Oh?"

"It's not a big deal. Really."

"Why don't you come in and let me put something on that. It's the least I can do after you stood up for Brock and drove him home. If you get something on it now, it might stop your face from being rainbow colored in the morning."

"It'll be okay. I'm used to wearing the pride flag's colors."

The joke fell flat. Kane stared at Jake, his expression solemn. "Why don't you just come in and let me help, Jake?"

"All right, but I can't stay long." Damn it, why couldn't Kane be an asshole? It was so much easier to refuse people when they didn't act like they gave a shit.

Kane stepped back and gave Jake some room to exit the truck. He stepped down onto the pavement and shut the door, pocketing his keys as he followed the other man up the cobbled walkway. Although he tried to pay attention to what he was seeing, he barely noticed anything other than the way Kane's ass moved under his shorts. When Kane opened the screen door and held it, Jake tore his gaze away from the other man and pointed to the rock garden running alongside of the house. "That's nice. You do it?"

Kane shrugged. "It came with the house."

"Oh." So much for trying to make small talk. Jake stepped up onto the concrete stoop and walked inside. He hovered just inside the door and looked around, while Kane continued into the kitchen. Everything looked different than he remembered, smaller. He wasn't sure what he'd expected in way of decoration; the clean space he viewed certainly wasn't it. He supposed part of him anticipated the house to look exactly the same as it when the McPhersons had lived there.

The main entrance opened into a small foyer with a large living room directly ahead. To his right was a set of stairs leading to the second floor. On his left was the open doorway through which Kane had disappeared. Jake could see a small dinette set made of dark wood, traces of chrome appliances, and a white countertop inside the eat-in kitchen.

Not wanting to follow Kane into the kitchen, Jake moved toward the living room and glanced around. A low-slung, cream sofa with built-in side tables sat facing a large entertainment center packed with stereo equipment and a flat screen TV. DVDs and CDs filled the shelves. An espresso finish on the wooden surfaces created a sense of balance when joined with the lighter shades of the couch and the cream-colored area rug beneath it. The wall at the back of the room was painted a vibrant red, a symbol of good luck, and offset the monochromatic colors of the furniture. Jake thought it was a nice room, though he could live without the red.

A single closed door loomed at the back of the living room. If Jake remembered correctly, that door led to the master suite, which would now be Kane's bedroom. He wondered what it looked like. If Kane slept surrounded by decadent silks and mounds of lush pillows, or snuggled beneath an old patchwork quilt on a plain double bed.

"If you're looking for something kinky, I keep the torture rack and all my whips and chains in the basement."

Lost in thought, Jake jumped and whipped around to find Kane grinning at him. "Very funny."

"Sorry. I just couldn't help myself. You looked so serious, like you expected to be walking into a dungeon."

"Well, I remember how much you used to love those BDSM pornos we shoplifted from the video store."

"Oh, God. I'd forgotten all about that." Kane groaned. "Do not let Brock hear about half the shit we did as kids. I'd never hear the end of it."

"I bet." To fill the silence, Jake said, "The house looks nice. Different than I remember."

"Well, yeah, I would hope so. Do you remember that awful furniture the McPhersons had, with the big green and orange flowers?"

"Oh, yeah. They even had green shag carpeting to match. Whoever thought puke green and orange was a good combo should've been shot. That stuff was hideous."

"Definitely." Kane held out a bag of frozen peas. "Here you go. These should do the trick for that eye."

Jake accepted the bag, his fingers sliding against Kane's as he took hold of it. "Thanks."

"No problem. So, do you want to sit down or something? I was just watching the race from earlier today when you showed up. I taped it."

"I guess that means you don't want to know who won, then?" Jake teased him.

"It's not like I can't guess, but I'd rather you not ruin it for me."

"All right.

They moved to the sofa and sat down, Kane on one end and Jake on the other. Kane picked up the remote and turned on the NASCAR race, the sounds of revving engines and sports commentary filling the gap in conversation.

Jake settled against the cushions and leaned his head back, resting the peas over the right side of his face. The icy cold made his bones ache, but it would help keep the swelling down, no matter how uncomfortable it felt now. Yawning, he closed his eyes and listened to Kane shout at the drivers, wondering how long he had to sit there before he could make his excuses and leave. With Kane being so nice to him, Jake felt the least he could do was make an attempt not to be an asshole.

The next thing Jake knew, something nudged his shoulder. He was warm and comfortable, and he didn't want to move. He was having the most delicious dream about Kane. They were young again and at the lake, sunbathing by the water. The sun shined down on them, bathing them in heat as they rolled around in the grass and kissed, happy just to make out and rub against each other. Like they used to do, before things got so complicated.

"Jake. Hey, Jake? Wake up, Sleeping Beauty. You're snoring like a buzz saw and drooling on my couch."

Groggy, Jake lifted his heavy eyelids. As his eyes focused, he saw Kane leaning over him, their faces inches apart. Relaxed by sleep and horny from his dream, Jake let instinct take over and leaned forward, covering Kane's mouth with his own. Kane gasped and his lips parted, giving Jake the opening he needed to slip his tongue inside and rub it over Kane's. He sipped from the other man's lips, tasted the sugary sweet taste of soda and something darker, muskier, that was all Kane.

Jake groaned and pushed the kiss deeper, angling his head for just the right fit. Kane shifted beside him, one hand moving in to frame Jake's face as he moved closer. Side by side, Jake reached out and ran his hands over Kane's broad shoulders and down his arms. The smooth skin rippled under his touch, the fine hairs abrading Jake's palms as he caressed the corded muscle of Kane's forearms.

"You taste good," Kane said, running a line of tender kisses down Jake's throat. "Even better than I remember."

Kane discovered a particularly sensitive spot right under Jake's jaw that made him shiver, goose bumps littering his skin. Jake angled his head back and held still, basking in the feel of Kane's wet lips on his skin until the urge to squirm grew too high.

"Christ, I missed this," Kane mumbled into Jake's hair.

"What?" Jake asked, nuzzling his way down Kane's throat to the soft curve where neck met his shoulder. Below, the copper discs of Kane's nipples beckoned him closer, the tiny buds hard and in need of his attention. "Making out on the sofa? We just did this the other day."

"No," Kane panted, kissing the side of Jake's face. "Not making out, smartass." He nipped Jake's earlobe and soothed the sting with his tongue. "This. Us. Together again."

Jake stiffened at the reminder of their past; he stilled, his mouth against the hollow beneath Kane's Adam's apple. His pulse thundered in his ears, the sound of his ragged respiration suddenly louder as the implications of what he was doing hit home. Seconds ticked by while he remained frozen, desire warring with his conscience.

Kane pulled back and gazed down at Jake with passion-glazed eyes the color of pine trees at sunset. "You okay?"

"I'm fine." Jake pulled Kane's head down and kissed him, trying to shrug off the sense of unease. He tried to lose himself in the taste and feel of Kane   in the silky skin underneath his fingertips, in the shift and play of Kane's back muscles rippling as Jake caressed the depression between Kane's shoulder blades. The other man smelled of clean sweat and the heady musk of testosterone—the alluring aroma perfuming the air as their desire rose higher.

Kane broke the kiss to run his lips over Jake's jaw. "You feel so good. Even better than I remember."

All right, Jake thought, I've had enough. "Could you just not talk? It's killing the mood."

Kane jerked away and sat back on his calves, his forehead wrinkled. "Are you going out of your way to be an asshole, or does it just come naturally now?"

"What?" Jake shivered and rubbed his hands over his arms, missing the heat and weight of Kane's body atop his. "I'm sorry. I'm not trying to piss you off. I just…" Jake rubbed his palms over his forearms, trying to warm himself. "You keep bringing up shit from the past, like it has some bearing on what we're doing now, and it's fucking with my head."

"I don't get it, Jake. I just made a couple of little comparisons. What's the big deal?"

"That's the problem. There is no similarity between now and then."

Kane stared at Jake as if he'd sprouted horns. "How do you figure that? No matter what's happened between then and now, we're still the same people."

"No." Jake sat up, putting further distance between them. "You might be, but I'm not."

"Maybe we shouldn't do this." Kane folded his legs underneath him and sat facing Jake. "I want you, Jake, but you're blowing hot one minute and cold the next. It's giving me a headache."

Jake snorted. There had to be a joke in there somewhere something tawdry about housewives and headaches, or something crude involving blowjobs—but he didn't feel like thinking about it long enough to come up with one. It would probably lighten the mood. It just wasn't worth the effort when his brain felt like a spinning top. "I want to finish what we started, but only if you can leave the past where it is. It has no bearing on now."

"I'm not sure I can do that. You're asking me to pretend we've never shared anything. That I don't remember how things used to be between us."

"We were just stupid kids. We didn't share anything, except our dicks." So what, if that wasn't quite true? It was painfully obvious that Kane hadn't shared his feelings back then, not after what he'd done, and Jake wasn't about to lay his emotions bare.

"That's bullshit, and you know it." Kane's eyes narrowed. "What we had was special."

"Yeah," Jake said sarcastically. "So special you told everyone I was a freak who begged to suck you off until you gave in because you felt sorry for me. There's a memory to cherish."

Kane grimaced. "I don't know what kind of rumors were spread after I left, but I never said that. I wouldn't have."

"Just drop it."

"I swear, Jake, I didn't say anything like."

"I said drop it. I don't want to talk about the past or what you did. It's a dead-end subject."

"How many times do I have to apologize? I made a mistake. I'm sorry I hurt you   that's the last thing I ever planned to do   but I was young and stupid and scared. Why can't you understand that and forgive me?"

"Because I loved you, damn it! You were my whole fucking world, and then you just shit on me and left me behind to clean up the mess you made." Jake snapped his mouth shut and dropped his gaze to his lap, desperately trying to curb the wall of emotion building inside him. His nose burned. His vision wavered, his eyesight blurry.

Christ, what was he thinking, blurting that shit out? He sounded like a whiny pussy.

"You think I had it so easy after we moved?" Kane said softly. "Being watched all day and night. Sitting through church sermon after sermon, while my parents tried to have the homosexuality preached out of me. Having to pretend I liked girls, putting on an act for so many years that I damn near started to believe the ruse myself. That's how Brock came about, you know? His mother was one of the girls I pretended to care about so my parents wouldn't suspect me of being anything other than the perfect, all-American jock they wanted." Kane's jaw tightened.

Jake blinked and bit the inside of his cheek. What had happened to Kane after he'd left Blacksburg had never crossed his mind. Sure, from time to time he'd wondered about where Kane was or what he was doing, but he hadn't ever considered that anything bad might have happened to the other man. He'd assumed Kane was living the good life somewhere, oblivious to the crimp he'd put in Jake's.

"God," Kane continued. "They actually seemed relieved when I told them Sherry was pregnant. There we were, barely more than babies ourselves at seventeen, and my father insisted we get married right away. I think he honestly believed that would be the best thing for me. Thank God, Sherry's parents wouldn't hear of it. They wanted more for their daughter than being a teen bride, stuck to a troubled kid like me, who they didn't imagine would amount to much after graduation."

"Why didn't she just…" Jake zipped his lips shut, not sure how well Kane would take it if he finished the thought out loud.

"Have an abortion?"

Jake nodded.

"Sherry didn't believe in it. She wasn't religious or anything, but she said she couldn't go through with it. She planned to have him and then give him up. Instead of letting her put the baby up for adoption, my mom agreed to help raise him until I got through college and could take care of him on my own. Her willingness to help me with Brock is probably the only reason I didn't turn my back on them and take off right after high school. With Mom's assistance, I was able to attend night classes in business management at the community college, work during the day, and keep my son."

Hearing about how rough things had been for Kane didn't make him feel any better. Instead, the thought of Kane's suffering in silence, with no one to turn to for comfort, lodged in his brain and began to fester. At least Jake had been able to commiserate with his brother. Kane had been forced to hide and internalize his emotions.

"I didn't know," Jake murmured inanely, not knowing what else to say. He felt like shit, selfish for not once considering what Kane may have had to overcome. Maybe Logan was right when he said Jake was self-absorbed.

Kane smiled sadly. "Well, now you do."

Jake reached out and ran his fingers over the back of Kane's hand. He'd always loved Kane's hands; the way he could hold his strength in check and use such gentleness when the occasion called for it. "Maybe I should go."

"You don't have to." Kane twined his fingers with Jake's and gave them a squeeze. "You can stay, if you want."

Jake met Kane's gaze, trying to read the other man's mind through the elusive quality of his deep green eyes. Failing, he sighed. "I don't know." He wanted to, he really did, but he wasn't so sure it was a good idea. He kept sticking his foot in his mouth and making things worse. God only knew what would come spewing out next.

"Shh." Kane scooted closer and leaned in, pressing his lips to Jake's a tender kiss. "This doesn't have to be complicated. I want you to stay. Please?"

Chapter Seven

How they went from staring at each other one minute to in each other's arms the next was a blur of movement and frenzied kissing. Jake found himself pinned to the soft couch cushions, Kane's hard body holding him down while his tongue plundered the recesses of Jake's mouth. He looped his arms around Kane's shoulders and held on tight, his mind on a permanent loop-the-loop of want and need. He wasn't sure how smart it was for him and Kane to keep yo-yoing back and forth between fucking and fighting, but he would take it.

"Bedroom," Kane gasped, pulling away. "Brock's upstairs."

Right. Jake had forgotten all about the kid. He nodded and rose on shaky legs, trailing behind Kane. As they walked into the bedroom, his kept his eyes locked on the other man's tight ass, watching it sway beneath the loose blue shorts.

He wanted in that ass. *Bad.*

Jake paused as Kane crossed the room and turned on a small lamp, illuminating the area around the bed. Kane was backlit by a pale glow as he shoved down his shorts, revealing the thick length of his cock and heavy balls surrounded by a soft wreath of dark brown curls.

Moisture pooled in Jake's mouth as his gaze moved over Kane's body: the firm pecs, the slanting oblique muscles, the prominent jut of his hip bones. The potential Kane's body had shown as a teen had more than been fulfilled. The rugged physique before him was all man.

Was he really going to do this?

Making love with Kane was probably a huge mistake, something he would most certainly regret later. He could no more deny his need than a thirsty man without a sip of water. One more time with Kane wouldn't be enough to quench his hunger, but Jake would take what he could get. He wouldn't ask for anything more.

Kane sat on the edge of the bed, his face clouded with uncertainty. "You coming?"

God, yes. Probably sooner than I should, if I'm not careful.

Jake nodded and pulled his T-shirt over his head, dropping it to the floor as he walked toward Kane. He popped the top button on his leathers and left the rest as they were, intrigued by just how far Kane would play along with what he wanted to do. Stopping in front of Kane, Jake grasped the other man's hands and led them to the stiff outline of his cock. "Take them off me."

Kane didn't argue. Nimble fingers worked to open the buttons and pushed the leather pants down over Jake's hips. He watched Kane's face as he discovered the black jockstrap and licked his lips.

"Fuck, that's hot." Kane trailed the back of his fingers over the mesh pouch. "I always did like you in a jock."

Jake shuddered from Kane's words as much as the light touch, his dick swelling even further from the attention. The tip strained against the elastic band, trying to break free of its confinement. "Go on," Jake prodded. "Take my cock out. Touch me."

"My pleasure." Instead of pulling aside the jock, as Jake had expected, Kane leaned forward and ran his cheek over the pouch. He mouthed Jake's dick through the mesh, following the line of his cock all the way to the top, where he now extended above the fabric. "Mmm, you smell good."

"Uh-huh," Jake mumbled, his gaze fixed on Kane's head at his groin. "I taste even better."

"Bet you do, but I can't just take your word for it."

Jake chuckled. "Help yourself."

"Don't mind if I do."

Kane's finger slipped under the elastic and pulled the jock out and down, freeing Jake's cock. He gripped it right below the head and stroked downward, pulling Jake's foreskin all the way back to reveal the slick crown. Bending closer, Kane blew a stream of humid air over the wet tip, making Jake shiver and lock his knees.

Tension ratcheted higher as Jake watched Kane extend his tongue then flick it over his slit, licking the copious amount of precum clinging to his cockhead. He wrapped his warm, wet lips around bulbous crown and sucked, his tongue probing the slit.

Jake rocked his hips, trying to feed more of his dick into Kane's eager mouth. "That's it. Suck me."

Kane looked up at Jake, and their gazes connected. His stare didn't waiver as he lowered his jaw and swallowed Jake's cock. Air rushed from Jake's lungs as he felt the tip of his cock being squeezed by Kane's throat muscles. When Jake was sure he couldn't take another second of the viselike pressure around his crown, Kane slowly backed off. His tongue pressed against Jake's flesh all the way up until only the head remained in his mouth. "Jesus, Kane. Where'd you learn how to do that?" On second thought, he didn't really want to know.

Thankfully, Kane ignored his question. "Like that, do you?"

"God, yes," Jake said, his gaze trained on Kane's mouth and the way it had made his shaft glistened with saliva.

"Good," Kane replied and began to tongue the hypersensitive ridge of Jake's crown through the cowl of his foreskin. He dipped his tongue into the slit, making the nerve endings in Jake's crown zing, before swallowing him back down to the root. Kane's head bobbed up and down, bathing him in wet heat followed by agonizing suction. The hand around the base of Jake's shaft worked in concert with Kane's mouth. It threatened to drive him insane.

Unable to take much more, Jake held back his orgasm through sheer willpower. His balls ached to fire their load. He didn't want the pleasure to end so soon but any more of the sweet friction, and he would be spilling himself down Kane's throat, instead of buried in his tight ass.

That was out of the question.

"Stop," Jake whispered.

Kane backed off of Jake's cock, the bulbous tip resting against the pout of his lower lip, and looked up.

The utter look of pleasure on Kane's face went straight to Jake's balls. "Lie back on the bed."

"All right," Kane said with a nod. He scooted away from the edge and moved into the center of the bed. Lying on his back, he lowered his legs until they were flat against the mattress. Jake stepped away and bent to take off his boots. He pushed his pants and underwear all the way down then stepped out of them.

Naked, Jake joined Kane on the bed, stretching out beside him. Propping himself up on one elbow, he returned Kane's hungry gaze and leaned in closer. Kane met him halfway, their mouths meshing with renewed need. Long, languid kisses rolled from one into another. Kane's mouth was delicious, the perfect blend of soft and slick, his tongue a whirling cyclone against Jake's.

Running his hands over Kane's chest and arms, Jake explored the smooth contours of skin over hard muscle and bone.

He let his fingers dance, circling the stiff crests of Kane's nipples, and followed the hard bridge of sternum down to the taut peaks and valleys of Kane's abdomen. The muscles jumped under his fingers, Kane's abs rippling in the most alluring way.

Jake slanted his upper body over Kane's while keeping their mouths fused. Unable to think about anything other than how good Kane tasted, Jake held on tight as a maelstrom of sensation bombarded him. He rubbed up against Kane, his cock like iron where it pressed into Kane's hip. Against his side, Jake felt the proof of Kane's desire, the wet tip of Kane's cock dragging over his skin, leaving a slick path wherever it touched.

So fucking good. How could kissing get him so hot, so fast?

Jake kneed open Kane's thighs, making a slot for himself at the center of Kane's body. He pressed their groins together, searching for just the right fit, the perfect alignment for their cocks.

Kane welcomed him down, enfolding Jake in his arms. Calloused hands kneaded his flesh as Kane lifted his legs and locked his ankles at the small of Jake's back, his rough heels digging into the top of Jake's ass.

They rutted—pushing and pulling against each other—until Jake's breath came in a ragged gulps, and his heart pounded under the force of his desire. One scorching kiss spiraled into another, with no distinction as to where one began and the other ended. Their tongues dueled, gliding on the slick lubrication of their saliva. It made Jake's cock ache, his need for more building with no clear path to release in sight. He refused to spill himself outside Kane's body. Didn't think he was above begging, if that's what it took.

Judging by the way Kane panted and thrust against him as if his life depended on how much sensation his cock received   Jake figured Kane wanted it just as badly as he did.

Gasping, Jake wrenched his mouth away. "I want you now, Kane. Please, baby," he whispered, desperate. "Let me fuck you."

Kane blinked up at him with heavily lidded eyes, his face flushed, and lips swollen. "Yes." He grasped his legs, pulling his thighs against his chest. "Do it. Fuck me, Jake."

Backing up, Jake rose onto his knees. With trembling hands, he lined his prick up with the tender whirl of Kane's asshole and pressed inward. He looked down as the slick crown of his cock spread Kane open and swore, jerking away. "Fuck."

Jake sat back on his heels, frustrated with himself and his lack of control. No one made him forget a condom. Never. The desire he felt for Kane was a dangerous fucking thing. Something he'd have to worry more about, when his dick wasn't full to bursting and his balls didn't ache with the need to unload.

"Jake?" Kane let go of his legs and leveraged himself up on his elbows. "What's wrong? God, don't tell me you're going to back out now. I'm dying here."

"No." Jake shook his head, trying to instill some sense back into his brain while he was at it. "We just need a condom. Do you have any in here?"

"Oh. They're in the top drawer of the nightstand. Lube's in the same place."

"Great." Jake leaned over and fumbled through the drawer until he located a dented but full box of condoms and a well-loved bottle of Astroglide.

Necessary items in hand, Jake took his place between Kane's widely splayed thighs. He ripped open the condom wrapper, poured a drop of lube in the reservoir for that extra slick feeling around his foreskin, and quickly rolled the latex down his steely shaft.

Still lying on his back, Kane watched Jake's every move with hungry eyes. "So we're good to go now?"

"Almost." Jake slicked his fingers, using more lube than was necessary. With his dry hand, he patted Kane's leg. "Up you go."

Kane nodded and bit into the plump flesh of his lower lip. He pulled his legs up against his chest, opening himself to Jake's eager gaze. The position lifted the firm mounds of

Kane's buttocks and parted his cheeks, revealing the crease between and the tiny entrance Jake sought.

With two lube-slickened fingers, Jake circled Kane's anus and exerted gentle pressure. A fraction at a time, he slid his fingers inside Kane's body. Up to the second knuckle of both digits, Jake cast a glance at the other man's face to gauge his reaction.

Kane caught his gaze and held it, his lips parted as breath puffed in and out. Maintaining eye contact, Jake shoved his fingers home the last little bit and twisted them, searching...

"Fuck, yes." Kane's back bowed, and a flush spread up his neck. "Right there."

Bending at the waist, Jake leaned forward and licked Kane's balls, running his tongue over the bristly, baby-soft skin. To the accompaniment of Kane's moans, Jake continued upward. He laved the full length of Kane's thick shaft and flicked his tongue over the tip, unable to resist the opportunity to taste his lover.

"Stop." Kane bucked, jerking away. "God, stop. I'm going to come if you keep that up."

Jake grinned against Kane's flesh, tempted to draw the torture out a little longer just so he could watch Kane writhe for him. Unfortunately, he was just as ready as Kane. His dick actually hurt it was so hard; the fragile skin was swollen beyond its usual breadth.

Kane grunted as Jake pulled his fingers free. "Hurry. Fuck me."

Jake just nodded, beyond coherent speech as he lined his prick up and pushed. After a second of minor resistance, Kane's sphincter relaxed and gave way, allowing the head of Jake's cock to pop through. Right away, the tiny ring of muscle closed around him. Kane's channel gripped Jake's dick like a fist. He groaned and shut his eyes, willing himself to breathe.

Ever so slowly, he pushed deeper, trying to take his time and allow Kane to get used to his girth. Kane's hands smoothed down Jake's sides and reached around to cup his ass. Fingers dug into Jake's skin, pulling him down as Kane's hips rocked upward, sinking the full length of Jake's cock deep inside Kane's clasping sheath.

"Fuck." Kane's back arched, his head pushing into the mattress.

Jake stilled, looming over Kane. "Are you all right?"

God, he didn't want to stop—he would, if he was hurting Kane—but he damn sure didn't want to. Kane's ass hugged his dick like a glove. Even through the latex he could feel Kane's body rippling around, tightening, and letting go.

"Yes, I'm fine." Kane wiggled his hips. "Move, darlin'. Give it to me."

Darlin'. Jake rolled his hips, pulling halfway out before sliding deep once again. Christ. He hadn't heard that word directed at him with Kane's inflection in just short of forever. Amazing how one little word could make him feel like a king.

Jake pressed his toes into the comforter for leverage and gave Kane his all, fucking him in long, hard thrusts. The bed springs squeaked, adding a harmony to their panting breaths and occasional grunts.

"Oh God…Jake." Kane tilted his head back and squeezed his eyes closed, his neck straining. "So close…don't stop…"

Jake leaned forward and pressed a clumsy kiss to Kane's parted lips. "I won't." He grimaced as the slick walls around his cock tightened, making it that much harder to keep from tipping over the edge into oblivion. "Come on. Give it up for me. Come on my cock."

Kane whimpered, his head tossing from side to side. "Please…just a little more… Harder."

Sweat dripped into Jake's eyes as he picked up his pace. Hair whipped around his face and caught on the moist contours of his cheeks and neck, sticking there unabated while he put every last vestige of energy he had into giving Kane exactly what he wanted.

The channel around Jake's dick clamped down, undulating around him like live silk as heat sprayed between their sweat dampened bodies. Jake's toes clenched against the comforter, his back stiffening. He thrust home once and then again, burying himself to the balls as his cock jerked within the tight clasp

133

of Kane's body, filling the condom in short, hard spasms. Tremors passed through Jake's body, going on and on until he wasn't sure he could survive another. He'd never come so long or as hard in his life. The contractions were so drawn out it felt like his balls were pulling the very marrow from his bones. Through it all, he held onto Kane like a drowning sailor hugging a buoy.

Finally, the tremors subsided, leaving Jake limp and slack-jawed, while Kane petted his hair. He nuzzled his face against Kane's throat, too exhausted to speak, and breathed in the satisfying scent of sweat and sex on the other man's skin. He knew he'd have to move in a minute, to get rid of the condom if nothing else, but he would have been perfectly happy to stop time in that instant and spend the rest of his life right there, lying in Kane's arms. He opened his mouth, ready to say as much, before he realized how stupid and clingy it would sound.

With a snap of his jaw, Jake reached between their bodies and held the condom secure as he pulled out. He rolled to the side of the bed and disposed of the condom, pitching it into small wastebasket next to the bed.

The bed shifted and a hand touched down on Jake's shoulder. "You okay?"

"Mm-hmm," Jake turned his head and summoned a smile for Kane. "Better than okay." Just a little freaked out at how badly he wanted to curl back over on the bed and start from square one all over again. Which was so far outside of the realm of normality that it worried him. He didn't spend the night with his erstwhile lovers, and he certainly didn't stay for the awkward mornings.

Kane brushed his lips across Jake's cheek and reached passed him to grab a hand full of tissues off the nightstand. "Can you stay?" he asked, while swabbing cum from his stomach.

No. Definitely not. "Maybe for a little while."

"All right." Kane pitched the tissues and lay down, patting the bed beside him. "Come over here."

Even though he knew he shouldn't, Jake crawled back onto the bed and into Kane's waiting arms.

Chapter Eight

After his interview on Monday afternoon, Jake played tourist in Washington, D.C. He wandered in and out of the various museums and spent a few hours looking around. Having time alone, without being watched by the town busybodies or being stopped on every street corner to talk, was a luxury he didn't have at home. He'd even turned off his cell phone, content to just loiter with only his thoughts for company.

He liked the anonymity that came from being in a larger city, but he wasn't sure if the job was right for him. Everything else aside, the lack of freedom to pick and choose his own clients bothered Jake. He'd never been one to follow orders easily. The stuffed shirts who ran the firm were adamant about the image they wanted to project. It didn't broker much leeway. They would be in charge of what styles he could use, and everything else was to be avoided.

After looking through their portfolio of work, it appeared to Jake as if ninety percent of their business was centered on country chic and classic elegance. Neither suited his taste, nor would they give him the challenge he thrived on. Part of the fun of being an interior designer was moving from one project to the next, being able to mix things up and always having something new to work on. Decorating variations of the same room over and over would get old quick.

It didn't help that he found himself thinking about Kane more than once while he was being questioned and introduced to the other members of the firm. One minute he'd been fine, jabbering away about his preferences for this or that, and the next, he was lost in thought, recalling the way Kane looked or felt, the way the tiny laugh lines around his eyes relaxed and smoothed out while he was asleep.

The sun was just beginning to set as Jake hailed a cab and rode back to his hotel, his thoughts in turmoil. The interview had gone well, and Jake was confident there would be a job offer in his future. Whether or not he decided to take them up on the position, he'd wanted to make a good impression. Being scatterbrained wasn't the notion he'd wanted to imprint.

On one hand, he had a chance to start a new, exciting life rife with promise. On the other, he had a stable, if not booming, business he loved and the possibility of a relationship with a man he could easily fall for, if given the chance.

No doubt, Kane was probably still pissed at him for skipping out while the other man had been sleeping early Monday morning, but that would probably be easy enough to smooth over. He'd had his reasons for leaving. If he'd stayed, Kane would have wanted to talk about what had happened between them and what it meant, if anything. Jake simply didn't have the answer.

He still didn't.

All he knew was that Kane made him feel things no one else had.

Jake felt wanted, as if such a thing were even possible after so little time together. He couldn't explain it. Even though he was nervous and unsure of himself around Kane, Jake had the unflagging sense that Kane saw through the coat of polish he presented to the rest of the world right down to the very essence of who he really was. The notion was both eerie and comforting.

The more Jake thought about it, the less he knew what to do.

What he decided, as he paid the cabbie and made his way into the hotel, was that he needed a little relaxation. A night out, with no goal other than to have a few drinks and sweat away some of his tension on the dance floor.

* * * * *

Solo in a sea of writhing bodies, Jake moved to the rhythm of the music, his mind blank of everything except the burn in his muscles as he swayed to the intoxicating beat. Even over the thundering rhythms, he felt the echo of the crowd's siren call   each man joined in a singular endeavor to lure in and claim their chosen prey for the night. Jake, on the other hand, was content merely to dance.

The club he'd chosen, The Park, was one of the largest in the area. It boasted two floors, each complete with a dancing area and its own bar. When he'd arrived at half past nine, he'd been surprised to find a line already forming outside. From the other establishments he'd been to, Jake had assumed the place would be virtually empty that early. He was wrong.

After waiting forty-five minutes to get inside, Jake was ushered into a cavernous room, packed from wall to wall with bodies. The music was loud, but not abrasively so, an eclectic mix of top forty hits and classic disco favorites. He'd walked through, just looking around to see what was what, and could honestly say The Park was the most impressive nightclub he'd ever been in.

Setting an almost festive mood, tiny glittering blue and white lights ran across the upper molding of the rooms and along the baseboard, adding a bluish tint to the dim interior. Pure white lights marked the stairs to the upper floor. Blue highlighted both bars and raised platforms, where go-go boys danced in G-strings no bigger than dental floss.

Men came and went, sidling up to him with lecherous grins, only to quickly move on once they realized he wasn't interested in being groped and virtually fucked through his clothes on the dance floor. Although there was a banquet of nubile flesh to choose from, men to fit practically any taste, he found himself oddly unaffected. His dick was at half-mast inside the tight constraint of his jeans, but he was lax to do anything about it. It actually felt good to hang suspended in a prolonged state of minor arousal. Almost as if he were waiting for something special that had yet to happen.

A new song began, something with a throbbing pulse and a little slower than others. He measured his pace, swaying to the tempo, and wiped the sweat from his brow. The crowd around him thinned out as people heading for the bar until a more up-beat song came on. Jake stayed right where he was. He enjoyed the scenery and the endorphin rush that came from physical exertion. He'd have to take a break for water soon, but not quite yet. Not while everyone else was swarming the bartender with orders.

Jake's neck prickled a second before someone slithered up behind him, a warm body rubbing up against his ass. Intrigued, he put an extra twist in his hips, pushing his ass back against the other man's groin. Although he wasn't really in the mood for more, it was fun to tease. A nice ego-boost to be wanted.

Turning his head to the side in order to tell the man he wasn't interested, Jake was captivated by sparkling blue eyes underneath an artfully arranged mop of bleach blond hair. He snapped his mouth shut, considering his options. As he turned to get a better look, the man backed off a few steps and grinned, nodding toward the back of the room. Without another word, he strode in the direction of the backroom. Jake stared after him, drinking in every inch of his retreating form   the tall, lanky body and firm, round ass encased in tight, faded jeans.

In the blink of an eye, Jake envisioned how things would play out with the other man. Jake would follow him back to an appropriate dark corner inside a tiny overcrowded room that would probably smell like stale cum and sweat. Amid a plethora of guttural grunts and moans from the men around them, they'd proudly display their equipment and size each other up. From there, things would move quickly. They'd grope each other and kiss, or maybe not—some men were strange about kissing. After an obligatory stroke or two, Jake would spin the other man around and fuck him where he stood leaning against what was probably a dank cement wall. In less than the time it took to have a pizza delivered, Jake could get off and be on his way, with one more meaningless conquest under his belt. Yet another orgasm that left his balls as empty as his heart.

Is that really what I want?

Someone bumped into Jake from behind, making him stumble forward. As he righted his balance and glanced around at the wall of bodies shaking and grinding to the music, Jake realized this wasn't what he was wanted. There was nothing wrong with casual sex—it served a purpose—but he needed more.

No matter what happened with Kane, whether they could work things out between them or not, he was done with the party scene. Even the prospect of being alone sounded better than being surrounded by vain, preening men who were only interested in a quick orgasm.

Winding his way around people left and right, Jake made a beeline for the exit. He stepped out into the gloomy night and exhaled, as if a weight had lifted off his chest. The clarity that came from finally realizing what he wanted out of his personal life made the job decision easy.

He was going home, where his friends and family were. He might never be a millionaire, but at least he could be in charge of what he did and when. He could make his mark on the world on his own terms, without anyone breathing down his neck to do things their way.

Several cabs sat against the curb, waiting for club patrons to come out. Jake headed toward one and hopped in, giving the cabbie his hotel name. Sitting in the back, he turned on his cell phone to check his messages. There were several from Logan, all saying the same thing. In the last, his brother's voice sounded strained, his tone tight as he barked for Jake to pull his head out of his ass long enough to call home, that it was urgent.

Worried, Jake dialed Logan's number and listened to the phone chirp in his ear. Glittering lights passed in a blur outside the window.

"Hello," a sleep-roughened voice whispered into the phone.

It took Jake half a second to recognize who it was. "Hey, Aaron. Sorry to call so late, but Logan's message sounded important. Is he awake?"

"No, but hold on and I'll wake him up."

Jake heard something rustling and then Aaron telling Logan to take the phone.

"Jake?"

"Yeah, it's me. What's up?"

"Are you sitting down?"

"Yes," Jake said. "Why? What's going on?"

"I don't know how to candy coat this, so I'm just going to spit it out. There's a rumor going around that you forced yourself on someone."

"Yeah, so? That's not exactly news. People have been talking about it off and on for years. I guess Kane moving home after all this time has stirred things up again."

"No, this is new. It isn't about what happened when you were a kid. We'll get it sorted out, but you need to come first."

"No." Jake said, shaking his head, even though part of him knew Logan couldn't see him. "Kane wouldn't do that to me. Not again."

"It's not Kane this time. Does the name Jimmy mean anything to you?"

"Fuck."

"I take it that's a "yes"?"

"Yeah, but I didn't force him to do anything. You know better than that, Logan."

"I know, but that doesn't change what's going around. When are you coming home? I don't have to tell you that the sooner you get this taken care of the better."

"I'm on my way. Just…" Jake rubbed his eyes, his mind spinning. "Shit. I don't know. I'll be on the first flight I can arrange."

"All right, Jake. I'll see you when you get back."

"Thanks, bro. I'll see you soon." Jake hit the end call button and stared out the window, tired beyond measure. He should have been pissed off; part of him was, but a larger part was just exhausted by all the drama. When did it ever end? It seemed like something or someone was always conspiring to bring him down just because he preferred dicks to tits.

His decision to quit playing the field couldn't have come at a better time. As soon as he got this situation straightened out—and he damn well would—he was going to start keeping to himself. It just wasn't worth it.

Chapter Nine

By the time Jake's flight landed, he was fit to be tied. Rushing through the terminal, he picked up his bag at the luggage carousel and hurried out of the airport. It was an hour-long drive back to town, and he wanted to get there yesterday.

After sitting in the terminal all night, swilling coffee, and waiting for something to open up on standby, he'd lucked into an available seat on the five a.m. flight out of D.C. It was just as well that he'd stayed there instead of returning to the hotel, since there hadn't been a snowball's chance in hell of him being able to rest anyway.

A million different outcomes plagued him, exacerbated by what little he knew of the situation. Logan hadn't said anything about charges being filed against him, but who knew what the kid was thinking.

Finding his truck where he'd left it in short-term parking, Jake climbed aboard, pitched his bag on the passenger seat, and set off for home. The sooner he got this whole mess resolved, the better. He'd gone through this shit once before, and he'd be damned before he went through it all again. No longer was he a naïve kid ready to hang his head and pray things would resolve on their own.

He wasn't sure of where to find Jimmy, but he didn't let that deter him. There was one man who would know exactly where to find the little bastard.

After whittling down the hour-long drive into just under forty-five minutes by speeding as much as he dared, Jake exited the interstate and drove passed Sam Goode's home. To his disappointment, the driveway was empty, the old man's Blazer nowhere to be seen.

There was only one other place Jake knew to look—Time and Again. Surely, the old man wouldn't go in to work after having his grandson come forward with such startling news. Jake knew the allegations against him were bullshit, but Sam wouldn't be aware of that.

Figuring he would hit another dead end, but unwilling to give up before he'd resolved things, Jake drove downtown and parked on Main Street. The gloom and doom he felt wasn't reflected by the sunny day. Everything looked normal; people walked in and out of the various stores and window-shopped.

Jake stormed up the sidewalk, brushing passed two older women who gasped and jumped out of his path as if he carried leprosy. As he approached the store, he noticed the red and white sign on the door was turned to open. Through the plate glass window, Jake saw Sam standing behind the counter, a dust rag in hand as he wiped down the area around the register.

Steeling his resolve, Jake stormed into the shop, letting the door slam shut behind him. A riot of twinkling bells went off overhead, announcing his arrival.

Sam's head jerked up, a pair of wire-rimmed spectacles perched on the bridge of his hawkish nose. His eyes narrowed as he spotted Jake walking toward him. "You have a lot of nerve showing your face around here after what you've done. Why I ought to—"

"Where is he?" Jake spat, cutting off the older man. He stopped on the opposite side of the counter and glared. "Where is that lying sack of shit you call a grandson?"

"Why you…you… How dare you come in here and start making demands." The old man lifted his hand and waved his bony finger in the directions of the door. "Get out. Right now, before I call the police and have you forcibly removed."

"Call whoever you like. I'm not budging until you tell me where I can find Jimmy." Jake took a deep breath and let it out, while reminding himself that no matter how much he wanted to snarl and curse at the other man, Sam didn't know Jimmy was lying. The fact that they'd never particularly gotten along before this mishap was beside the point. "I just want to talk to him, Sam." And possibly wrap my fingers around his neck until he turns blue and spills the truth. "I know you don't like me, but I didn't do what he's saying. I wouldn't."

"Why should I believe that?"

"Because it's the truth."

"Are you calling my grandson a liar?" Sam's nostrils flared. "Jimmy wouldn't make something like this up. He's a good boy."

"Regardless of what you think, I didn't take anything that Jimmy wasn't willing to give. We fucked; it was not rape!"

"Get out!" Sam's cheeks filled with fire. "Get the hell out of my store this instant."

"It's all right, Pops."

Jake's attention zipped beyond Sam, where Jimmy stood over the threshold leading into the backroom. The outrage he felt dimmed in view of the red, puffy cast to Jimmy's eyes and the gaunt pallor of his face. He stood with his shoulders hunched inward, his gaze downcast, nothing like the scheming trick Jake had envisioned. If anything, Jimmy appeared smaller somehow, and more upset than Jake felt. He wasn't sure what to make of that, but one thought blasted through his mind, clear as day.

What right does he have to cry when it's my life he's fucking up?

Sam rushed to Jimmy's side and tried to usher him back into the other room. "You shouldn't be up here, Jimmy. I can take care of this."

Jake caught Jimmy's gaze and tried to hold it, failing as the younger man's attention dropped to the floor. He spoke up before Jimmy let himself be herded away. "I think he needs to stay right where he is, Sam."

Sam glanced at him, shooting daggers with his eyes. "You stay out of this and keep your mouth shut. You have no right—"

"No right to what? Your grandson claims I forced myself on him—which is complete and total bullshit—don't you think that gives me the right to question him?"

"Ignore him," Sam said to Jimmy, turning his back on Jake. "Why don't you go home? You shouldn't have come in with me today."

"No," Jake said, smacking his hand down on the counter. "I want some answers, damn it."

Jimmy jerked, but stayed silent.

143

"Why would you do this? Say these things that we both know aren't true. I'm sorry if I hurt your feelings by not accepting your calls, but in no way does that excuse what you've been saying about me." Jake leaned across the counter. "Look at me!"

"All right, I've had enough of this." Sam picked up the handset of the cordless phone and brandished it like a knife. "I'm not going to tell you again. Leave."

Jimmy kept his gaze down and whispered, "I'm sorry."

"That's not good enough," Jake said, ignoring the old man in favor of looking at Jimmy, trying to compel him to explain through sheer force of will. "I want to know why. Why lie about this and then not follow through with pressing charges? What do you have to gain?"

Jimmy looked up and opened his mouth, floundering for a second before he snapped it closed.

Sam frowned. "You should be thankful he hasn't pressed charges against you. I tried to talk the boy into going to the police, but he wouldn't hear of it. Didn't want to be embarrassed by having to admit what you did to him."

"Would you get a clue? He didn't want to go to the police because it isn't true, God damn it!" Jake felt like howling in frustration. Instead, he skirted around the counter and grabbed Jimmy by the collar of his shirt, forcing the other man to finally look at him. "You have to tell the truth, Jimmy. Please."

"I…" Jimmy's eyes were wild as he glanced from Jake to his grandfather and back again. "I don't know what you want me to say…"

Sam slapped at Jake's arm with the phone. "Get your filthy hands off him."

"Back off," Jake snarled, keeping his attention focused on Jimmy. "Admit it, Jimmy. For God's sake, tell him I didn't rape you."

"I'm not going to let you bully my grandson into lying for you, you deviant bastard. I'm dialing the sheriff's station right now. I wouldn't stick around long enough for them to arrive if I were you. Who do you think they'll side with? After all, this isn't the first time you've taken advantage of someone. I remember how you molested the Sharp boy when you were in school. I'll see to it that Jimmy files charges and puts your ass behind bars were you belong. You can spend the rest of your days seeing how it feels to be on the other side of the buggering."

"Grandpa," Jimmy gasped. His face drained of color as his wide-eyed gaze darted from Jake to his grandpa. "I never said anything about filing charges. I just   "

"Hush, Jimmy. Of course you're going to file charges. None of this is your fault. No one will blame you; you'll see." Sam paused, seeming to concentrate on the phone against his ear. Then he said, "This is Sam Goode at Time and Again Antiques. I need to have an officer come remove an interloper from my store. Yes, ma'am, I've tried to make him leave, but he just won't listen." A frown creased Sam's brow. "Fifteen minutes? You can't get someone here sooner? Oh, all right, that'll be fine then. Thank you." He set the phone down and smirked at Jake.

"Please, Jimmy," Jake pleaded, his desperation growing. He knew he was in the right, but that didn't mean it wouldn't come down to his word against Jimmy's if the police were brought in. With his shady past, it was hard to fathom whether a jury would believe Jake's side of the story. Even from his point of view, Jimmy seemed like a more believable character. "You have to come clean now, before this goes any further. I know I was wrong to ignore you the way I did, but do you really want to take this to court and see me put in jail over it?"

A bell above the door jangled, heralding someone's arrival, just as Sam piped up. "Damn right he wants to see you behind bars for what you've done. You may have gotten away with this once before, but I can guarantee you won't be so lucky this time."

Logan and Aaron walked into the store, followed by Kane, who said, "That's not quite true, Sam, and you damn well know it. We've already had this discussion once."

Jake had never been happier to see anyone in his life. "What are you guys doing here?"

145

"I saw your truck pull in and called your brother." Kane nodded at Logan. "I figured you might need a little moral support."

Touched more than he cared to admit, Jake simply nodded. "Thanks."

Kane looked at Sam, his eyes narrowed into emerald slits. "Jake never forced me to do anything, which I already explained to you yesterday, after I overheard you spreading your rumors in my restaurant."

"Of course you'd lie for him now." Sam sneered. "He probably has you brainwashed to believe whatever he wants. You should have stayed away from here, like your parents wanted. They were smart for getting you away from him and all his perversions."

Jake opened his mouth, ready to ask Sam if he thought all gay men had the ability to brainwash people or if he just thought Jake was that special, when Kane spoke.

"You're wrong." Kane shook of his head. "I hid who I was for years, out of fear my parents would look at me differently. Out of blind panic that they would cast me out into the street like trash if they knew I was gay. They could have moved me to Antarctica, and it still wouldn't have changed who I am or made me stop loving Jake."

Kane's gazed at Jake, his expression so earnest it made something inside Jake's chest tighten to the point of pain. His lungs felt as if all the wind had been sucked out of them.

"You can save your breath." Sam glared at all of them. "The police are already on their way, and they'll sort everything out when they arrive. I would advise you to be gone before they get here, unless you'd like for me to press charges against you all for loitering."

Logan stepped forward. "You can make all the idle threats you want, Sam. I seriously doubt anything would come of your petty loitering charge." He shot Jake a look of commiseration as he pushed passed Sam and approached Jimmy. In the patented "grown-up" voice Jake had heard every time he'd done something wrong over the years, Logan said, "Son, don't you

146

think it's about time you admit the truth so we can put this all behind us before it gets any more complicated?"

Jimmy cast a glance at his grandpa. "I'm sorry, Pops. Jake didn't force himself on me. I made it up."

"What?" Sam asked, clearly flabbergasted. "But what about the things you said? Why would you lie to me about something so serious?" He shot a wary glance at Jake and the others. "I don't understand."

"I know," Jimmy said. "I wasn't thinking."

The kid paused, appearing to clam up again, and Jake had had enough of being patient. "You're going to have to do better than that," he demanded. "I want to know what possessed you to do this."

Jimmy gulped. "I…when I found out Pops had installed a surveillance camera, I freaked out. Then, when I couldn't find the recording, I knew I had to do something. I couldn't just let him watch the tape and see the…things I'd done with you."

"What?" Jake asked, his heart thudding in his ears. It wasn't as if he'd forced himself on anyone or had anything to hide really, but he didn't like the thought of a video of his naked ass floating around out there somewhere for someone to find. "There's a video?"

"No," Jimmy shook his head. "There wasn't a tape. I found out the camera was just for show after I told Pops what happened. I thought if I said I didn't like it, that you coerced me, Pops would let it go. I thought that he would want to keep what'd happened quiet, so I wouldn't be an embarrassment to him."

Jimmy rapidly blinked, his eyes shinning with moisture as he transferred his attention to his grandpa. "I didn't want you to think I was like all the men you put down for being gay. I…" He swallowed. "I never wanted to you to find out. I know how you feel about homosexuals." He looked down at the floor, his voice barely above a whisper. "I don't want you to hate me too."

"I believed you. I stood up for you. And this is how you repay me?" Sam's round face turned an unflattering shade of crimson. "I can't deal with this right now. I don't even want to look at you." He stormed out of the room, walking outside just as a panda car pulled up in front of the shop.

Logan patted Jake on the shoulder. "I'll walk outside and make sure he isn't saying anything outlandish to the police. Don't be long, all right?"

"Sure," Jake said. "Thanks for coming, bro. It means a lot."

Aaron, who'd stayed silent through the entire exchange, walked over to Jake and hugged him. He gave a tight squeeze and scampered after Logan, leaving Jake, Jimmy, and Kane standing in front of the service counter. Kane wandered across the aisle and pretended to study a rolltop desk.

Jake stuck his hands in his pockets and looked at Jimmy. Paths of sluggish moisture streaked down other man's cheeks. Even though he didn't really want to, Jake felt sorry for him. "So, um, are you going to be okay?"

"Yeah," Jimmy hiccupped. "I'll be fine."

God, this is nerve-wracking. He'd never been good at awkward situations. This had to be the worst he could think of. "Well, I guess I should be going."

"I really am sorry," Jimmy whispered. "I never expected things to get this out of hand."

"It's over now." Jake shrugged, his gaze searching out Kane's. "In the end, you told the truth, and that's what counts."

* * * * *

After parting ways with Logan and Aaron, Kane left his restaurant in the hands of his employees and followed Jake home. Although Jake didn't want to be a burden, he was happy for the company. As an added benefit, it allowed him to be alone with Kane so they could talk.

He was more nervous about the upcoming conversation with Kane than he had been about confronting Jimmy. He felt justified about that, even if he hadn't known the outcome. With Kane, he wasn't sure about anything.

His palms were sweaty, and his mouth was dry. The pit of his stomach felt like he'd ingested battery acid. Leftover adrenaline from earlier—the by-product of high-strung emotions and an anticlimactic resolution—flooded his system, with no outlet in sight. Throwing up wasn't out of the question. He had to remind himself to breathe as he unlocked his apartment door and stepped inside, with Kane right behind him.

"Would you like a drink?" Jake asked as he closed the door behind them.

"I'm good, thanks." Kane crossed the room and sat on the sofa.

"Okay." Jake joined him on the sofa, sitting close. His arms ached to reach for the other man; his fingers itched to twine with Kane's. Instead, he folded his hand in his lap. "So, thanks for calling Logan and showing up when you did. It was thoughtful of you. Probably more than I deserve after the way I ran out on you." Turning sideways, he met Kane's gaze. "I'm sorry about that. I'd like to try to explain, if you're willing to hear me out."

"It's all right." Kane shifted until he was facing Jake, his back against the couch arm. "We didn't exactly make any promises. You don't owe me anything."

"I feel like I do." Jake sighed and brushed his fingers over the soft khaki material covering Kane's thigh. "Since you've come home, my brain has felt like a scrambled egg. I keep screwing everything up and pushing you away, because what I felt for you wasn't easy. It couldn't be solved by fucking or fighting, and I didn't know how to deal with it. It was easier just to chalk it all up to hormones and say the hell with it."

Kane laid his hand over Jake's and gave it a squeeze. "It's okay. Really."

"Let me finish." Now that he'd started, he wanted to get it all off his chest before he lost his nerve. "Ever since you moved away, I've played the field. It's no big secret that I've slept around. I kept things casual because I thought that was better, less messy than building a relationship that was doomed to fail anyway. But the truth is I was afraid to let anyone get too close to me. I didn't ever want to be vulnerable enough to feel the kind of pain I went through with you."

"Oh, baby." Kane's eyes filled with sympathy. He leaned closer and brushed his lips over Jake's in a tender kiss. "I'm so sorry."

Jake's pride flared at the pity reflected in Kane's expression, but he did his best to crush it, and continued. "I'm not trying to make you feel bad; I just want you understand where I'm coming from. Why it's been so hard for me to see through the forest to the trees. I thought by staying detached from the people around me that I could control my fate, but I was wrong. All I've done is use people and deny myself a chance for something genuine, for what I really want."

"What is it, baby? What do you want?"

"Did you mean what you said earlier?" Jake swallowed, his mouth dry as cotton. Fear gripped him by the balls and squeezed as he waited for Kane's response.

Kane gazed at Jake for one, long unnerving moment. Finally, he nodded. "I meant every word. I've never stopped caring about you, Jake. You were my first love. I imagine a part of my heart will always belong to you."

Thank God, Jake thought. He grasped Kane's hands, kissed the moist flesh of one palm, and pulled him closer. Kane scooted toward him until their knees bumped. Jake bent at the waist, and Kane met him halfway, closing the distance between them, as their lips came together. He kept his eyes open and locked with Kane's as the kiss slid into a slow, languid glide of mouths and tongue. When he reluctantly pulled away, Jake's stomach rolled with tension. "What if I want more than a part?"

Kane's gaze lowered, his thick lashes shading his eyes. "What exactly are you saying?"

Fuck, it couldn't be a good sign that Kane wouldn't look him in the eye. "What if I want it all? What then?"

"What about that job offer?" Surprise must have registered on Jake's face, because Kane went on to explain. "When I couldn't find you, I called your brother to warn him about what I'd overheard Sam saying in the restaurant. He told me where you were."

Jake still couldn't believe Kane had gone out of his way to help him, not after the way Jake had treated him, but he wasn't above looking a gift horse in the mouth. Kane's good heart was one of the things Jake had always loved about him. "I'm not taking it. Everything I want is right here."

Kane tsked, his eyes smiling. "That was pretty risky. What if I'd said no?"

"Then I would have followed you around like a puppy until you changed your mind, or had a restraining order taken out to keep me away."

Kane laughed and kissed him, a quick smack of the lips that only wetted Jake's appetite for more. He caught Kane by the nape, preventing him from pulling away and kissed him again. Kane's lips softened on a quiet moan that was more air than sound and parted under Jake's. Slipping his tongue through the oval of Kane's mouth, Jake explored the pearly surface of Kane's teeth and the sharp edges before sliding his tongue over and around Kane's with long sweeping licks. Kane tilted his head, taking the kiss deeper as their tongues dueled. He gripped Jake's shoulders, kneading the tense muscle. By the time they came up for air, both of them were panting; Kane's face was flushed with desire. Jake's cheeks felt hot, so he figured he was probably in the same condition.

"Well," Kane said, taking a deep breath, "I guess it's a good thing I didn't say no."

Jake wanted nothing more than to strip Kane bare and make love to him, but he needed a solid answer first. "Is that a yes?"

"Maybe."

"Only maybe?" Jake faked a pout, knowing how silly he looked with his lower lip pouched. "You can't do any better than that."

Kane pushed Jake back against the sofa and climbed into his lap, straddling his legs. He lifted his shirt over his head and tossed it behind him. Bare chested, the scrumptious muscles of his chest and abdomen on display, he gripped the hem of

Jake's shirt and tugged it up and off before leaning forward and cupping Jake's face in both hands. He smiled as he caressed Jake's stubbled jaw with his thumbs. "Where's the fun in that? This way you have to work to convince me."

Jake nipped at Kane's thumb and let go, tilting his head back to look up at Kane. "That sounds promising, but just for safety's sake, how would you propose I do that? I'd hate to take a chance on screwing things up before they've even begun."

"Hmm," Kane said, pretending to ponder his choices. "I'm not sure." He rubbed the pad of his index finger over Jake's lower lips. "How much is it worth to you?"

One word summed it up. "Everything."

"Oh." Kane's eyes softened. "Good answer."

Jake grinned. "I thought so."

"Smartass," Kane said with a hoot.

"I'm your smartass, though," Jake teased, nervous but more than ready to finally let go of his fears and face whatever the future held in store for them.

"Yeah," Kane agreed as he leaned down, his mouth hovering over Jake's. "You are mine."

As Kane's lips closed over his, Jake couldn't help but think the future had never looked sweeter.

The End

About Amanda Young

Amanda Young is a multi-published romance author. Since she tends to write whatever strikes her whimsy, all of her novels fall into various subgenres. Among her titles you'll find contemporary, manlove, and paranormal.

The stories she writes are bold and usually push the boundaries of what's acceptable. Basically, she writes stories about men and women who love indiscriminately and wholeheartedly. Her characters are never perfect; they're flawed and oftentimes troubled. Which makes it that much more satisfying when they receive the happy ending we all deserve. No matter what genre her books fall into, she can guarantee they'll end with a happily ever after. In her opinion, it's just not a romance without one.

To learn more about Amanda, please visit her website: http://www.amandayoung.org.

Proof

Made in the USA